THE PHLEBOTOMIST

Ella Road

THE PHLEBOTOMIST

OBERON BOOKS
LONDON

WWW.OBERONBOOKS.COM

First published in 2018 by Oberon Books Ltd
521 Caledonian Road, London N7 9RH
Tel: +44 (0) 20 7607 3637 / Fax: +44 (0) 20 7607 3629
e-mail: info@oberonbooks.com
www.oberonbooks.com

A catalogue record for this book is available from the British
Library.

PB ISBN: 9781786824530
E ISBN: 9781786824547

Cover image by rocksunderwater

Printed and bound by 4edge Limited, Essex, UK.
eBook conversion by CPI Group (UK) Ltd, Croydon, CR0 4YY.

ELLA ROAD
WRITER

Ella trained as an actor at The Oxford School of Drama after her English degree at Somerville College, Oxford. *The Phlebotomist* is the first play she's written. She is currently under commission from Theatre Royal Plymouth, and is further developing her play *Roosting* following an R&D scheme at the Park Theatre. She is also developing work for screen. She is co-founder of the new writing company Flux Theatre and is a Soho Theatre Young Writer.

SAM YATES
DIRECTOR

Theatre work includes *Glengarry Glen Ross* (Playhouse, West End); *Desire Under the Elms* (Sheffield Crucible); *Murder Ballad* (Arts – nominated for three WhatsOnStage Awards and Olivier Award for Best Supporting Actress); *Cymbeline* (Sam Wanamaker Playhouse/Shakespeare's Globe – Ian Charleson Award commendation); *East Is East* (West End/UK Tours); *The El Train* with Ruth Wilson (Hoxton Hall); *Outside Mullingar* (Ustinov Studio, Bath); *Billy Liar* (Manchester Royal Exchange – winner of the Manchester Theatre Awards for Best Actor and Best Newcomer); *Cornelius* (Finborough/59E59 Theaters, NY – nominated for four Off West End Theatre Awards and Critics' Pick The New York Times) and *Mixed Marriage* (Finborough).

Film work includes *The Hope Rooms* (winner of the Rhode Island International Film Festival 2016 Grand Prize Filmmaker of the Future Award); *Cymbeline*; *All's Well That Ends Well* and *Love's Labour's Lost* (The Complete Walk, Shakespeare's Globe) as well as two music videos, *Emeralds* and *Auld Wives* for the Ivor Novello Award-nominated band Bear's Den (Communion Music).

Radio work includes *Ecco* (Radio 4).

CAST AND CREATIVE TEAM

JADE ANOUKA
BEA

Theatre work includes *Cover My Tracks* (Old Vic);
Shakespeare Trilogy (Donmar at King's Cross); *Doctor
Faustus* (West End); *Julius Caesar, Henry IV* and *The Tempest*
(Donmar/St. Ann's Warehouse, NY); *So Here We Are* (Royal
Exchange/High Tide); *Chef* (Soho); *The Vote* (Donmar);
Omeros (Sam Wanamaker); *Clean* (Traverse/59E59, NY);
Romeo and Juliet and *Hamlet* (Shakespeare's Globe); *Moon
on a Rainbow Shawl* (National Theatre); *Romeo and Juliet*
(Bolton Octagon); *Wild Horses* (Theatre503); *Love's Labour's
Lost* (Shakespeare's Globe/US Tour); *Blood Wedding*
(Southwark Playhouse); *Twelfth Night* (York Theatre Royal);
The Taming of the Shrew and *The Merchant of Venice* (RSC); *The
Penelopiad* (RSC/NAC, Canada) and *Handa's Surprise* (Little
Angel Theatre).

Film work includes *Baby Gravy, The Dark Channel, A Summer
Hamlet* and *A Running Jump.*

Television work includes *Trauma; Chewing Gum, Lucky Man;
The Vote, Shakespeare Uncovered; Doctor Who, Secrets and Words*
and *Law & Order: UK.*

VINCENT EBRAHIM
DAVID

Theatre work includes *Dara* and *Behind the Beautiful
Forevers* (National Theatre); *Bad Roads* and *The Djinns of
Eidgah* (Royal Court); *The Empress* (RSC); *The Great Game*
(Tricycle/US Tour); *Occupational Hazards* and *Nathan the
Wise* (Hampstead Theatre); *Credible Witness* (Royal Court
Upstairs); *Ramayana* (Birmingham Rep and National
Theatre); *A Midsummer Night's Dream* (Tara Arts/Lyric);
Tartuffe, Little Clay Cart and *Fanshen* (National Theatre) and
Real Dreams and *The Danton Affair* (RSC).

Film work includes *Allied; The Physician; Material* and
The Curse of the Were-Rabbit.

Television work includes *40 North*; *Casualty*; *Hoff the Record*; *Hollyoaks*; *Doctors*; *The Old Guys*; *Compulsion*; *The Kumars at Number 42*; *New Street Law*; *After You've Gone*; *Meet the Magoons*; *The Lenny Henry Show*; *Holby City*; *Bedtime* and *Doctors*.

Radio work includes *Tumanbay*; *Revelation*; *Oedipus the King*; *School Drama*; *Dark Fire* and *An Everyday Story of Afghan Folk*.

Audio podcast work includes *My Indian Odyssey*.

RORY FLECK BYRNE
AARON

Rory trained at RADA.

Theatre work includes *Anna Karenina* (Abbey); *King Charles III* (Wyndham's); *The Vortex* (Gate, Dublin); *That Face* (Landor); *The Lion in Winter* (Haymarket); *Disco Pigs* (Young Vic); *Cause Célèbre* (Old Vic) and *Antony and Cleopatra* (Liverpool Everyman).

Film work includes *The Foreigner*; *Vita and Virginia*; *Night of the Lotus*; *Tiger Raid*; *Vampire Academy: Blood Sisters* and *The Quiet Ones*.

Television work includes *Death in Paradise*; *Harlots*; *To Walk Invisible*; *Jack Taylor*; *Midsomer Murders*; *Damo & Ivor* and *Grantchester*.

Short film work includes *Inbox*; *Bodies* and *Untitled Blues*.

CHERRELLE SKEETE
CHAR

Theatre work includes *The Seagull* and *Jack and the Beanstalk* (Lyric Hammersmith); *Harry Potter and the Cursed Child* (Palace); *Three Days in the Country* and *The Amen Corner* (National Theatre); *The Wind in the Willows* (Royal & Derngate Theatre); *The 24 Hour Plays: Old Vic New Voices* (Old Vic) and *I and Silence* (Finborough). Theatre work whilst training at the Royal Central School of Speech and Drama includes *The Edge* (New Diorama); *Sold*; *King Lear*; *Love's Last Shift*; *There's no Place Like Home*; *A Midsummer Night's Dream* and *Three Sisters*.

Musical theatre work includes *The Lion King* (Disney Theatrical Productions).

Television work includes *Silent Witness*, *Doctors* (series regular); *Danny and the Human Zoo*, *The Five*, *Ordinary Lies* and *Call the Midwife* (Season 4).

ROSANNA VIZE
DESIGNER

Theatre work includes *The Almighty Something* (Royal Exchange); *Diary of a Madman* (Gate); *Yous Two* and *No One Will Tell Me How to Start a Revolution* (Hampstead Downstairs); *Myths* (RSC); *King Lear* (Shakespeare's Globe); *Girls* (Soho); *Coastal Defences* and *Infinite Lives* (Tobacco Factory Theatres); *Measure for Measure* (North Wall Theatre); *Low Level Panic* (Orange Tree); *The Earthworks* (RSC); *St Joan of the Stockyards*, *Dark Land Lighthouse* and *A Thousand Seasons Passed* (Bristol Old Vic); *FUP* (Kneehigh); *The Rise and Shine of Comrade Fiasco* (Gate/National Theatre Studio) and *The Picture of John Gray* (Old Red Lion).

Opera work includes *Don Giovanni* (Hampstead Garden Opera); *A Midsummer Night's Dream* (RSC/Garsington Opera) and *Il Furioso All'Isola Di San Domingo* (English Touring Opera).

Future work includes *Leave Taking* (Bush) and *Don Carlos* (Exeter Northcott/Southampton Nuffield/Kingston Rose).

ZOE SPURR
LIGHTING DESIGNER

Theatre work includes *Beginners* (Unicorn); *Elephant* (Birmingham Rep); *Collective Rage* (Southwark Playhouse); *Tiny Dynamite* (Old Red Lion – Offie 2018 nomination); *Festival Voices* (Ugly Duck, a warehouse space, London Bridge); *Phoenix Rising* (Smithfield Market Car Park, site specific promenade – Offie Finalist 2017); *Elton John's Glasses* (Watford Palace); *Skate Hard, Turn Left* (Battersea Arts Centre); *Hidden* (UK Tour); *Natives* (Boundless Theatre); *Good Dog* (Watford Palace/UK Tour); *School*

Play (Southwark Playhouse); *Muted* (Bunker Theatre); *Erwartung/Twice Through the Heart* (Hackney Showroom); *The Knife of Dawn* (Roundhouse); *Affection* (The Glory, Haggerston/Stan's Cafe at A.E Harris, Birmingham); *Bitches* (Finborough); *Torch* (Latitude/New Diorama/Big Belly, Edinburgh Underbelly); *This Evil Thing* (New Town Theatre, Edinburgh Fringe); *Handle With Care* (Site specific touring production); *Hookup* (Hackney Downs Studios/Outbox Theatre) and *The Boy Who Climbed Out of His Face* (The Jetty, North Greenwich/Shunt).

DUNCAN McLEAN
VIDEO DESIGNER

West End theatre work includes *Labour of Love* (Noël Coward); *Big Fish* (Other Palace); Matthew Bourne's *The Red Shoes* and *Cinderella* (Sadler's Wells); *Saint Joan, One Night in Miami...*, *Privacy, City of Angels* and Phyllida Lloyd's *Shakespeare Trilogy* (Donmar); *The Real Thing* and *All About My Mother* (Old Vic); *The Bodyguard* (Adelphi); *Shrek* (Drury Lane); *Derren Brown – Infamous* (Palace) and *Frost/Nixon* (Gielgud).

New York theatre work includes Matthew Bourne's *The Red Shoes* (City Center); *Privacy* (Public Theater); *The Tempest* (St Ann's Warehouse); *Let It Be* (St James) and *The Norman Conquests* (Circle in the Square).

Other International theatre includes *Starlight Express* (Germany); *The Bodyguard* (Worldwide); *Evita* (Worldwide) and *Ghost* (Germany).

Events work includes *The League Of Gentlemen – Live Again!* (UK Tour); *Harry Enfield & Paul Whitehouse – Legends!* (UK Tour); *The Sherlock Holmes Experience* and *The Game's Afoot* (Madame Tussaud's) and *28 Days Later; Dr Strangelove* and *Star Wars – The Empire Strikes Back* (Secret Cinema).

ALEX TWISELTON
SOUND DESIGNER

Work as a sound designer includes *The Trial*; *Oh My Sweet Land* and *Safe House* (Young Vic); *Story Fishers* (National Theatre); *A Man of No Importance Little*, *Shop of Horrors*; *Dangerous Corner*; *Anne and Zef*; *Stepping Out*; *Spread a Little Happiness*; *Epsom Downs*; *Blackbird*; *Death and the Maiden*; *A Taste of Honey*; *A Game of Love and Chance*; *The Country* and *Faith Healer* (Salisbury Playhouse); *Toro! Toro!* (UK Tour); and *The Girl in the Yellow Dress* (Theatre503);.

Work as associate sound designer includes *Network* (National Theatre); *Red Velvet* (West End); *A View from the Bridge* (Young Vic/West End/Broadway/LA/Washington DC) and *Our Country's Good* (Out of Joint US Tour).

Alex is currently a sound and video supervisor at the National Theatre.

LUCY HELLIER
CASTING DIRECTOR

Current work as a casting director on the following independent films includes *The Unravelling, Rendez-vous in Paradise* (Director Alain Berliner) and *War Wolf* (Director Simon West).

Other film work as casting director includes *The Ledge* (Director Howard J Ford); *All the Devil's Men* (Director Matthew Hope); *Soma* (Director Miklos Keleti) and *Medusa's Ankles* (Short film, director Bonnie Wright).

Film work as a casting associate includes *The Foreigner* (Director Martin Campbell); *Skyfall* and *Spectre* (Director Sam Mendes); *Iron Sky: The Coming Race* (Director Timo Vuorensola); *Stratton* (Director Simon West); *Billionaire Ransom* (Director Jim Gillespie); *The Confessions* (Director Roberto Andò) and *Tiger Raid* (Director Simon Dixon).

Television work includes *Knightfall*; *One Child* and *Borgia*.

Theatre work as a casting associate includes *Strangers on a Train* (Director Robert Allan Ackerman).

Prior to casting, Lucy worked for seven years as a senior sales executive in international distribution at ITV.

Thanks

To all the creatives who have shared their wisdom, especially Bethany Pitts, Jessica Norman, and my people at Flux. To all the actors who have given their time and energy. To Dr. Maryam Khostravi for her advice and encouragement. To Peter Clayton and all at the Criterion Theatre Trust. To Ramin Sabi at DEM. To the Hampstead Theatre for taking a punt on me. To Sam Yates for being amazing. To Sam Briggs, for showing me that biotech video in the first place. To Sope Dirisu, for always believing I could. And to my wonderful family and friends, for their invaluable support, love and inspiration.

'Doesn't everything die at last, and too soon?
Tell me, what is it you plan to do
With your one wild and precious life?'
– Mary Oliver

Characters

Bea: F (20s-30s, from the city)

Aaron: M (20s-30s, from the country)

Char: F (20s-30s, from the city)

David: M (50s/60s, from anywhere)

Interlude characters and voices: Various M/F

The company should reflect a diverse society. All roles can be played by actors of any ethnicity.

Interlude roles can be played by actors of any gender.

Notes on the Text

Interludes, including prologue, are written to be portrayed via multimedia (videos, screens, soundscapes, V.O.s, etc).

/   indicates an interruption.

…   indicates a broken or unfinished thought.

Act One

Present day.

ON SCREEN: Interview with chief medical officer SALLY DAVIES.

SALLY: / what I'm arguing is that right now, because of the cottage industry way we do these tests, we're spending a lot of money. And…and actually if we nationalise it and, well, run it properly we can get a lot more tests done and a lot better healthcare for people.

She clears her throat.

See the time for precision medicine is…well, it's already here. And if we want to keep our place at the forefront of global science we need everybody – staff, patients and public – to embrace its huge potential.

She takes a sip of water. Looks ahead confidently.

Within five years I want genomic testing to be as normal as, say, x-rays, or biopsies for cancer patients. I want to democratise genomics, democratise it so that it's available to everyone.

But that means we have to change the system. Right now, testing is exclusive. A luxury, really. It needs to be centralised and extended across the country. We need to take the science to the patients and not the patients to the science. This is about empowerment. I'm talking about knowledge. And, well, knowledge is power.

She smiles.

INTERLUDE 1

AUDIO soundscape. A&E. Muffled voiceovers:

DR 1: …just ran right out in front /

DR 2: ...by a tram, right outside the /

DR 3: Intracranial haemorrhage /

DR 1: Unconscious, suspected bleeding to the /

DR 2: Well do we resuss?

DR 3: What's the profile?

DR 1: Male, late twenties, no abnormalities, no record of /

DR 2: If we're gonna, we need to /

DR 3: Yes, yes, we resuss!

DR 2: Let's move him through please!

Soundscape fades into:

SCENE 1

Hospital hallway. About twenty years later. Background noise. BEA has just fallen on the floor. The trolley she was pushing is upturned. Blood vials roll in all directions. AARON is scrabbling around, picking them up.

A: Are you alright? Hey. Are you OK?

BEA makes a confused noise. Lifts her head.

B: Huh?

A: You alright? You /

B: Owh. Fuck. What...

A: You tripped, just /

B: Did you /

A: Fell.

B: What?

A: You fell over / Are you /

B: Oh God / What?

A: Quite hard. Are you alright?

B: Oh shit.

A: Is your head /

B: No, these, the bloods!

A: Don't worry, I've managed to get most of /

B: No, you shouldn't be handling those.

A: Oh. Sorry. Look, is your head OK?

B: How did I…?

A: You just dropped, like fainted?

B: I didn't faint. I'm not a fainter.

She stretches out her neck and winces.

A: Shall I get someone?

B: No.

She looks around at the vials.

I'm gonna get fired.

A: It's fine, no one saw.

He holds out his hand. She looks at him warily, then lets him help her up.

B: Ahh, nah, I think I…

She touches her head. Drops into a chair. Beat.

I'm really not a fainter, really not at all. Got a proper steady hand. God I feel like some Victorian lady, you know, 'fetch me the smelling salts'? Twat. Sorry.

He laughs. She reaches down to pick up a vial.

A: Sure I can't get you anything? Water?

She shakes her head.

What's your name?

B: Er Bea. Bea Williams?

A: Hi BeaBea Williams. I'm AaronAaron Tennyson.

He extends a hand.

B: Tennyson?

A: Yeah.

B: Like the poet?

A: Er, yeah.

B: Like Alfred Lord /

A: Yeah /

B: / Tennyson?

A: Er yeah that's the one.

B: You related?

A: Um. Um, Yes.

B: What? You serious? Nah you're shitting me.

A: Yes. I mean no I'm not shitt /

B: What like actually Alfred Lord the dude?

A: Yep.

B: We did 'In Memoriam' in school. I love it. It's like my favourite poem ever ever.

A: Really?

B: Yeah, no seriously, I. Like I didn't used to like English but then I. Yeah. It's beautiful.

A: It is.

B: I used to… Shit man. That's cool.

A: 'I held it truth, with him who sings, To one clear harp in
   diverse tones, That men may rise on stepping-stones,
   Of their dead selves to higher things…'

B: D'you know the whole thing?!

A: Ha no no.

B: Sounds good in your accent.

He smiles. Beat.

A: No one, um. No one's usually this enthusiastic about…

B: Oh I dunno, I just. See we did it in class 'round the time my
   mum passed and it kind of…well, yeah. All the stuff about
   moving onwards, upwards.

He nods.

A: And looking back, right?

B: Er… OK.

A: Clue's in the title.

B: Er, maybe.

A: I don't mean. I mean that's just what I…it's poetry,
   it's subjective, s'not fixed, that's the beauty right?

Beat. She stares at him.

B: Tennyson. That's mad.

Beat.

Sorry, I should really…

She gets up and goes to the trolley. Her head hurts.

A: Sure I shouldn't get someone?

*BEA shakes her finger, 'no'. Footsteps and muffled voices O.S. BEA
panics and tries to upright the trolley. AARON helps.*

DAVID, the senior porter enters.

D: Afternoon.

B: Hey. Hi.

DAVID picks a couple of vials off the floor.

D: Oh hello! I didn't recognise you for a... How are you?

He pats AARON on the back and smiles.

A: Oh, yes, sorry I didn't, um. Hi.

D: How you getting on?

A: Um, yeah, OK, yeah.

D: Glad to hear it.

A: Yourself?

D: Oh same old, same old, no complaints. All OK?

BEA nods and smiles.

Well. I'm on lunch. Do you two want anything from the...

BEA shakes her head and smiles.

A: Oh er no. Thank you.

D: Well, take care then.

A: You too.

DAVID does a strange little bow, then exits.

Beat. BEA laughs.

What?

B: I dunno.

AARON laughs.

He's... Do you even know him?

A: Not really.

B: Kinda weirds me out.

A: Yeah?

B: Not like, creepy, just…

She imitates DAVID's bow. AARON laughs. Then bows himself.

A: 'Take care'.

BEA snorts, picks up a vial.

B: Reckon he'll tell?

A: Who, the hospital mafia?

B: You joke yeah, but I'm new. They all bitch.

A: I'm sure he won't.

Beat. She carefully loads vials back onto the trolley.

So you're a big reader then?

B: Er, try to.

A: What kind of stuff?

B: Mmm…the romances? You know, Austen. Elliot.

A: The cheesy happy ever afters.

B: They're classics for a reason Lord Tennyson. I collect books actually.

A: Really?

B: Yeah.

A: Books, like real books paper books?

B: Yeah, I like being able to feel the pages. Bit nerdy /

A: No, that's cool.

Beat.

I collect money.

B: Ha, you tryin'a say you're rich?

A: No no, like old money, different denominations? I've got all the coins from like two hundred years. Kind of stupid.

B: Nah, that's...cool.

Beat.

Look, don't let me keep you.

A: I can't abandon you after you've 'swooned'. You're a damsel in distress.

She smiles.

So you're a...doctor?

B: Phlebotomist.

He looks blank.

Take the blood?

A: Ah, right. So nothing to do with bottoms then.

B: Er, no.

A: Disappointing.

She snorts.

B: So what you doing here Lord Tennyson?

A: That's a bit personal Ms Williams.

B: Oh yeah sorry.

A: Anal warts.

B: What?

A: I'm joking. Physio. Dodgy shoulder?

B: What is this, anal warts, bums, you five or what?

A: You laughed.

She smiles, then gets down and starts to count the vials. Her head really hurts. He brings some to her.

B: Thank you.

He checks around for more.

A: How many did you have?

B: God, dunno, wanna say like a hundred?

They carefully load them back onto the trolley.

This is a nightmare, gah, why didn't you catch me?!

A: What?

B: Isn't that what men are supposed to do? When women 'swoon'?

A: Sorry, didn't get the memo.

B: Honestly though, some of these are rating tests, management'll kill me if I've lost any. Ahhhh stupid shitty shoes, I must have just... I am *such* a *twat*.

A: Bea the clumsy phlebotomist.

She smiles.

Does that look like all of them?

B: Fuck knows. I mean I could just bang a couple of mine in and hope for the best.

A: What?!

B: Joking, obviously. That's messed up.

A: Well what's yours like?

B: What?

A: I just mean /

B: That's personal.

A: Sorry, if it's /

B: No, I mean, it's good. Like well above average.

A: Like what?

She looks at him coyly.

Well if it's good it's good.

B: Like 7.1?

A: That is good.

B: And yours?

A: Yeah it's er, it's pretty good.

B: Like what?

A: Need to get official certification but I'm looking at just below 9?

B: Wow.

A: You have to have over 8.5 to work in the city so /

B: The city?!

A: Yeah, I'm applying for bar training.

B: Eh?

A: Law. Gonna be a barrister.

B: Oh. Wow. That's. Wow.

Beat.

A: I'm not that into this whole ratings thing though to be honest.

B: No?

A: You know like all dating profile blood verification bollocks, shouldn't we just go for who we fancy?

B: Wow. Wow, yeah, no, I totally agree, that's. Yeah. But I can see why people wanna know. And anyway it's not just that is it, I mean the hospital's gone crazy with it. You should hurry up and get yours certified actually coz they're rolling out criteria in loadsa places and the queues are getting ridiiiiiculous.

A: Come and be sucked dry by you clumsy phlebotomists?

B: We're very gentle, promise.

AARON laughs. Beat.

I should go report this.

A: Why don't you just blame it on me? Tell them I wasn't looking where I was going, slipped over, I dunno. What are they gonna do? I don't work here, customer's always right.

B: You sure?!

He shrugs.

A: Are you hungry?

B: Starving.

A: That's probably why you fainted /

B: I'm not a / !

A: Alright, alright! When's your break?

B: Er /

A: We could go to one of those places across the road? That little yellow café looked nice.

B: What the one with the fruit? The fresh stuff? It's well expensive, it's all imported /

A: You could do with a pick-me-up after your 'swoon'. Some pineapple juice?

B: Pineapple juice?

A: Yeah they have big sign outside saying 'real fresh pineapple juice'.

B: Real pineapple juice.

A: Well…would you like some pineapple juice?

Beat.

INTERLUDE 2

AUDIO: NHS complaints helpline. Background noise of a call centre (maybe overseas). The HELPLINE ATTENDANT's voice is dead-pan.

HELPLINE: It's an opt-out scheme.

PATIENT: It's not clear enough.

HELPLINE: It was on the form, top left.

PATIENT: But I /

HELPLINE: May we remind you, you're under no obligation to disclose your /

PATIENT: Yeah, but *I* know now don't I? I went in there for an anaemia test. Iron. Then the guy comes back chatting about colon cancer! No pre-treatment for this strain anyway, I mean why would I want to spend the next decade knowing /

HELPLINE: I /

PATIENT: And do you know what's fucking ridiculous?

HELPLINE: I'm going to have to ask you not to swear.

PATIENT: I was this close to signing on a house. This close. Now they're giving me seven years max. What can I get with seven years mortgage? Shit all, seven years. Coz they know I'm not worth /

SCENE 2

Phlebotomy consultation booth. One year later. BEA sits beside a screen. CHAR paces. She has just had a blood test.

C: How long?

B: Couple more minutes.

BEA tidies away equipment.

C: Weird seeing you at work. Very professional.

B: Ha. Though, if you don't mind I'm gonna have to…

BEA pulls out a lunchbox and sits down.

C: Is that / ?

B: Yep. Cheap and nutritious, why change?

CHAR laughs, shakes her head. BEA eats.

C: Sorry for taking up your… Thanks so much for doing this.

B: Was waiting for you to ask to be honest. You're making the right decision.

C: It's not really a 'decision'.

B: Well you don't technically have to /

C: Yeah but not disclosing just looks worse doesn't it. Like you have something to hide.

B: Have you looked at other firms?

C: They're all asking, all the good ones anyway.

Beat.

B: Well it's amazing you've got this far at all isn't it? It's massive. That degree counts for something eh.

CHAR shrugs. Beat.

C: Jesus the tension's killing me! How do you stand this?

B: People normally wait outside, or come back next day. Stops it being so /

C: Horrendous?

Beat.

Sorry, sorry I'm being… I'm just feeling /

B: Come here. Look, whatever happens, I'm here for you OK? Whatever it is.

BEA checks. Still nothing.

You still seeing whats-her-face? With the hair.

C: Who? Oh. Nah nah, that was just…you know. Think I'm getting a bit sick of 'em to be honest. Might go back to men. Simpler.

B: Ha, don't know about that.

C: How is sexy Aaron? Sweet-smelling and louche?

B: Ha. Yeah he's great. We're good. We're er, well…it looks like we might move in together actually, so…

C: What?!

B: Yeah.

C: Fuckin' hell Bea. That's serious! Jeeeeeez! Well he is *awwwwfully charming.*

BEA smiles.

Though careful yeah, trust me, when you move in you'll probably find out all kinds of weird shit. I'm serious. My mate Marnie moved in with her man and it turned out he picked his nose right, and stuck it on the bottom of the kitchen table. Like she found bogies all over it. Think that's what clinched it in the end. That and the casual racism.

B: Ah fuck off he doesn't pick his nose!

C: Yeah and I bet he doesn't fart either.

B: Obviously he farts!

C: In front of you?

B: Um, sometimes, why?

C: No, that's a good sign. Keepin' it real.

B: Shut up.

BEA goes to flick CHAR. The device beeps. They both look at it. Beat.

BEA gives CHAR a look, 'Ready?'. CHAR nods.

C: No, hold on.

She takes a breath.

OK.

BEA goes to the screen, clicks and sees the results load. She swallows and scrolls down. CHAR watches her.

B: Um. Char.

Beat.

C: Don't fuck with me.

B: I'm not.

Beat.

C: What is it?

Beat.

Please.

Beat.

Bea.

Beat.

Bea?

B: I'm so sorry.

C: What is it?

B: It's the Huntingdon's. Everything else is fine, it's just /

C: Fuck! Fuck. No, fuck! Oh fuck.

B: I'm sorry. I'm really sorry.

C: God. Oh FUCK.

Pause.

How low is it?

Beat.

B: 2.

C: Let me see?

BEA shows CHAR the screen. CHAR tries to hold herself together.

B: Look obviously this is just a number. We can look through the breakdown? And then I'll book you in with a specialist to discuss what it means /

C: It means I'm unemployable. I'm nothing. I can't do anything.

B: Your general risk for cancers and most diseases is actually really low, which is really lucky, it's the /

C: Huntingdon's. Incurable. Yeah, I know.

B: But the overall /

C: I don't need the spiel Bea, I'm fucked.

B: Sorry. Sorry. I'm sorry.

C: How long have I got?

B: It's speculative, I'm not supposed to /

C: Yeah but everyone does, don't they.

B: It's just a rough /

C: Please.

B: I only take the blood, I don't normally...

CHAR looks at her. BEA reluctantly consults the breakdown.

Er... OK...er, well your predisposition to heart disease is also quite...but the Huntingdon's will kick in...soonish...so at a guess, lifestyle depending, you're probably looking at somewhere between eight to ten years.

C: What?

B: But obviously you have to take that with a pinch of, well, there are so many variables /

C: I /

B: Or you might get hit by a tram tomorrow! So you / Sorry /

C: Fuck / FUCK!

Beat.

B: I'll refer you to a genetic counsellor Char, this really isn't my /

C: I have a degree. And a masters. I have worked my fucking arse off, it's not fair!

B: It'll be alright.

C: No it won't, do you know what this means?!

B: I know what Hungtingdon's is, Char.

C: Dad stopped being able to walk /

B: I know /

C: Feed himself, hold things /

B: Stop it!

Beat.

Look. I'm gonna book you in with a counsellor. We need to start working out the best course of action for your disease.

C: I don't have a disease.

B: No, not yet, but…

Pause. BEA goes to her and hugs her. Silence.

C: Can you delete the file please.

B: What?

C: The results, the file, can you delete it?

B: There's no point, like you said, they're all asking, not disclosing just looks worse.

C: Please, just /

B: Deleting it won't change the result hun.

C: But if /

B: There's no point!

C: There is! Listen. Just bear with me yeah.

Beat.

I mean obviously I knew there was a fifty-fifty chance I'd inherit, but I never wanted to know, did I. But then criteria started appearing, and I knew it was a matter of time before I'd probably have to. So I started thinking about what I could do if things turned out…if I did have it. Started looking at how people get around it. And it's being done.

Beat.

B: What?

C: If we used someone else's blood, someone high, we could log it as me.

B: What?

C: If we used someone else's.

B: What are you asking me?

C: If there's someone high you've tested, we could, could we test that again in /

B: Sshh! I could lose my job.

C: I've thought this through.

B: Is that why you wanted me to do it? You said you needed moral support.

C: I did, I do. But I also thought if /

B: It's illegal Char. It's fraud. I can't, I'd lose my job. It's a good job, I can't.

   Beat.

   Sorry.

C: Are you enjoying this?

B: What?

C: Having the upper hand.

B: Don't be stupid.

C: I can pay you.

B: What?

C: I can /

B: No.

C: Dad left me a bit of /

B: Shut up.

C: I /

B: I don't want money.

C: Well, you do.

B: I'm fine, thanks /

C: Really?

B: What are you doing?

C: I know you're struggling.

B: Excuse me?

C: You're still paying off your mum's loans right?

B: I'm managing.

C: Porridge for lunch, and you could do with a new pair of /

B: You're blowing my mind right now, Char.

C: Don't fuck with me Bea, you used to take food from our fridge.

B: I.

   Beat.

C: It's OK, we knew /

B: Don't bring that shit up.

C: Sorry.

   Beat.

   Sorry, I didn't mean. I'm just… I really need this. I'll do anything, honestly. Please.

   Beat.

B: Look, I know how you /

C: No you don't! You're not low-rate!

B: No, but /

C: And Aaron, I bet he's high too, right? What is he?

B: Well he's…

C: What is he? Some poor low-rater? A little charity case? No, what is he?

B: You know you can't get a pupillage unless you're /

C: So what is he?

B: 8.9, but /

C: Wow /

B: But we don't care about ratings, we just met.

C: But you've both got good blood.

Beat.

Exactly.

Pause.

In the next few years I'm going to begin the slow process of falling apart. I'll get to a point where I can't work. Walk. Wash. I'll disintegrate. I need this job so I don't spend my last few years lying in a pool of my own /

B: OK! OK.

Beat.

Ok.

Long pause.

I tested a 7.7 woman this morning. Propensity for diabetes, something else minor. Nothing scary. Is that about right?

CHAR hugs her hard.

Give me a minute.

BEA exits.

INTERLUDE 3

ON SCREEN: A DATER records a video for a dating app.

DATER: Hiya, so this is me. I'm a bit nervous, so sorry if I stutter or whatever… So I'm average height. I'm bisexual so looking for all kinds of love really. Should increase my chances by 100%, or that's what mum says. Yeah don't really mind which one, boy or girl, just a person.

Nervous laugh.

Er, I work in marketing. It's really great. We're on the top floor and in summer I can get tanned on my lunch break which is just a massive bonus. I wear sun cream though, obviously. I mean I'm very careful. Ummm, this is my front obviously, side, other side. And check the uploads for party pics, gym pics, nude pics and there's a family pic there too coz I thought it was sweet and also thought you might wanna check out my fam? I look like Dad, so that's probably me at sixty. Ha. Er. Teeth are good.

Shows teeth. Then licks lips nervously.

Um…obviously you'll have seen I'm 5.4, but if you look at the breakdown most health risks are actually quite low. It's mainly brought down by IQ? And the fact that I'm allergic to peanuts. But apparently they're not that nice anyway, so. I also technically have 'addictive tendencies' but the only thing I really like too much is the gym, so I'm actually likely to have a long life? Unless I have a plane crash or something. But it hasn't happened yet, so. Yeah. Um. I guess if you've got this far then maybe you're interested in messaging me? Don't know what else to say really except I've always got good feedback from dates I've been on. Reviews are at the bottom.

Loses momentum. Finds it hard to look at camera.

Mum says I shouldn't worry about my rating coz I have a nice smile, so…this is me smiling…

Grins unconvincingly into camera.

SCENE 3

AARON and BEA's first flat. Six months later. AARON is studying in front of game show 'Wheel of Fortune'. Sound of theme music, crowd and cheesy V.O. BEA enters carrying a bag.

A: Where've you been? It's late.

B: What's this rubbish?

A: Er excuse me it's deep stuff, beardy guy just won a fridge freezer, look at his face, that's existential.

B: Close your eyes.

He turns it off and obliges. She takes out two huge blood oranges. He opens his eyes.

Beautiful right?

A: How much did they…?

She shrugs.

Bea!

B: I got a pay rise.

A: Yeah?

She kisses him.

B: Well go on then!

He peels one. They eat. The red juice runs down his chin. She giggles and wipes it.

A: Reminds me of when granny used to take us to the beach with a packed lunch.

B: Yeah?

A: More like an estuary really. Near her house. Tangerines and salmon sandwiches. I must have been about six, I just remember sticky, sandy hands.

B: Salmon?

A: Yeah.

Beat.

B: I've only been to the seaside twice.

A: Where did you go?

B: Brighton.

A: And?

B: Brighton. Went again.

A: Brighton's shit. We should find you some sand. Heard bits of Devon are alright.

B: Dunno, the whole South Coast sounds pretty dodge.

A: I'll protect you.

B: Oh yeah?

She tickles him.

A: No stop it. Stop stop, noooo stop it! Bea!

She pins him down.

B: What you gonna do?

A: No no, seriously, no, I swear I'll /

She tickles. He shrieks.

B: Erm what was that Lord Tennyson?

A: I'll, aaaaaah no no no, please, I'll watch episode seven without you!

She stops tickling. He pants.

B: You wouldn't.

A: You seen six yet?

B: When would I, I've been working!

A: If you don't get a move on I'll have to tell you how /

B: Nooo don't! I've been working! Don't!

She covers her ears. He scoops her up and plonks her down.

A: Well, he /

B: No! Seriously! Aaron!

A: You've got orange in your teeth.

B: If you tell me what happens I'll never do that thing again.

A: What thing?

B: The thing. I won't, no joke.

AARON mimes zipping his lips. He grabs her shoe.

A: Hello, what are these?

B: Nice aren't they?

A: Très chic.

He takes it off and rubs her foot tenderly. She relaxes, sprawling.

So beautiful when she's quiet...

She hits him. He leans over her.

'... I bent towards you, sweet in the air, in my arms, abandoned like a child...from your eager mouth, the taste of...'

He kisses her.

Oranges. 'Lean back again. Let me love you'.

B: Cheesy fucker.

A: You love it.

Pause.

Shall we get married?

B: What?!

A: I just thought. You know.

Beat.

B: You really asking me to marry you?

A: Yeah. Why not?

B: Your dad is why not.

A: You haven't even met him.

B: Exactly.

A: You're not low.

B: I know. I'm just saying…

A: Bea, my family's like me, they don't believe in all this rating crap, they won't even ask.

B: You're all super posh though aren't you?

A: Not really.

B: Salmon sandwiches?

A: That was years ago!

   Beat.

B: Next pay day I'm gonna buy an avocado.

A: You know it takes 160 litres to grow an avocado?

B: I know, and I'm gonna buy one and eat it naked in a full bath.

   AARON laughs. Pause.

   Suppose I better delete that MyRate profile then.

A: What?

B: Well couldn't take chances, there are some nice low 7s on there…

A: You actually / ?

B: I'm joking! Tool. Come here.

INTERLUDE 4

AUDIO: Radio charity campaign. Emotive Christmas music.

SPEAKER: …just can't get the vitamins they require. Diseases such as Scurvy, Pellagra and Beriberi are on the rise. Is it right for a child to be denied the basic vitamins they need?

For a small donation, you can give a child a portion of fresh fruit or veg every day for a week.

Malnutrition is one of the biggest contributors to health problems in the UK. We at Brain Food believe that everyone deserves a healthy start. If you agree, text FRESH to 6983, and revitalise a child this Christmas.

SCENE 4

Shop fitting rooms. Six months later. CHAR enters, out of breath.

C: Sorry sorry sorry, I got caught up in the march /

B: March?

C: Westminster. Anti-discrimination. It was packed, got – can I come in /

B: No I'm changing, wait!

C: You're not even dressed?

B: Well I *was* but then I... I had to choose veils on my own, the women was a right snotty cow.

C: Sorry, sorry! Do you wanna get some food?

B: No I'm gonna put it back on aren't I, I wanna show you!

CHAR sits.

C: Oh my gosh so you know Eddie Stone?

B: The singer?

C: Yeah, yeah, so he was there, coz he's quite active in anti-ratism right, and he kissed me on the cheek! He actually kissed me. Cross my heart. I'm not gonna wash it for YEARS. He's a proper sweetheart as well. You should have seen it, he stood up on a live national stream and came out.

B: As what?

C: 4.9

B: That's not that low.

C: No, but it's massive for the movement. His speech was so beautiful. And then he did that song, you know the one about the bird, you know 'Fly by me, little…something…', you know. I'm still buzzing, honestly.

B: You sound it.

C: Honestly, the atmosphere was amazing. I've been thinking lately /

B: Can you pass my shoes?

C: Er, sure.

She does.

But like I was sitting staring at those numbers at work yesterday, and I just thought, I had this feeling, like clock's ticking you know, properly ticking, so should I really be spending time sitting in that office?

B: What?

C: I've been looking into other stuff, something a bit more /

B: It's an amazing job though.

C: Yeah, yeah, I know /

B: Like an incredible job.

C: I know, it's just I've been reading this blog /

B: Right.

C: About self-worth.

B: Right.

C: And I think I could help people.

B: How long have you been there?

C: Eleven months, one week…two days.

B: Give it a bit more time.

C: I just /

BEA sticks her head around the door.

B: You have worked unbelievably hard to get to where you are. You've been to uni. Two fucking unis. People would kill for where you're at. I would kill for where you're at.

C: I know, but /

B: *(Whispering.)* I put my job on the line to get you there. Pass me the veil?

C: I appreciate that, but. I've been focused on getting into those shiny buildings since we was what, fourteen? But now I'm here. Now I have. I don't know… And do I want to work somewhere where I have to lie about who I am?

B: You're not lying about who you are, you're lying about who you will be, it's different.

BEA disappears back inside. Beat.

Have you told your mum yet?

Silence.

You need to.

C: I know.

Pause.

How you getting on in there?

B: My arse has grown in the last five minutes.

CHAR laughs. Beat.

C: You know the tests yeah.

B: Yeah.

C: They're sponsored right?

B: Yeah, different companies.

C: Right, and how do they frame it to you lot? 'We're going to give everyone a free predictive test because we're really lovely people?'

B: I dunno. It does make it accessible for /

C: The moment the insurance lot started asking I reckon the government should have put an end to it.

B: Well it allows for pre-emptive /

C: Yeah but who's gonna pay for the treatment?

B: Well /

C: Or what if it's not treatable?

BEA sticks head around the door again.

B: Look can you pipe down yeah, I don't wanna talk about this. I didn't ask you here for your I've been on some protest high horse bullshit, OK.

She disappears. Beat.

C: Sorry.

Beat.

Do I get to actually see you or…

B: I was waiting for you to stop talking.

Beat.

I can't do up the zip.

C: Show me.

BEA enters wearing a wedding dress. CHAR cups hand to mouth.

C: Oh my gosh! You look beautiful! Ohhhhhh Beeeaa! I'm gonna cry.

B: It's alright?

C: Honestly, you look like a princess! Here.

She zips her up and hums 'Here Comes the Bride'. BEA does a little shimmy. Beat.

B: Have a look at the price tag...

CHAR hesitates, then obliges.

C: Woah fuck me! Whatttt?! How will you /

BEA smiles.

B: It's OK. I've already paid.

C: How?!

BEA smiles coyly.

Aaron?

BEA shakes head.

What?

BEA grins.

What?

B: You can't tell anyone OK.

C: OK...

BEA looks around.

B: *(Whispering.)* So I might've started doing a bit of work on the side.

Beat.

C: *(Whispering.)* What. Blood?

BEA nods.

No. You badass! I told you it was easy/

B: It's not easy, it's risky. They've started monitoring our stats so I can only manage a few swaps a week /

C: This is mad!

B: We can't really talk about it /

C: You are such a sly biatch you know that.

B: Ssshhh! Look I've nearly paid off the loan now, just gonna do the wedding and make things a bit smoother then /

C: Does Aaron know?

B: Er. No.

Beat.

I exaggerated my pay rise. And um. I said that Mum left savings.

CHAR raises eyebrows.

Am I a terrible person?

C: Profiting off an obsessive ratist culture?

B: No, lying! Breaking the /

C: No. No. You're resourceful. His snooty fam can shove it up a their high-rate a-holes.

She shakes her head, smiling.

Bea, the black market biiiiiiaaattcch…

B: Ssshhhhhh!

C: I'm gonna rub my Huntingdons hands all over them at the wedding.

BEA snorts. Beat.

B: They won't be there.

C: What?

B: We've decided to just do friends. To be fair, I can't exactly /

C: Yeah but his are alive, no offence.

B: Only some weird cousins and his dad. And they live miles off, they're not tight. We thought it'd be easier if we just… we wouldn't get along anyway.

C: Which basically means they disapprove.

BEA shrugs.

That's bullshit.

B: I dunno. Guess it's a cultural thing.

C: No, it's a bullshit thing.

B: Look it doesn't matter. Fuck 'em.

C: Yeah. Exactly. Fuck 'em all. You're great. He loves you. And you look INCREDIBLE.

BEA smiles.

Just go knock on their door in this and they'll be like 'God DAYM she's a keeper'.

BEA sticks out tongue and goes back into cubicle.

B: Better work off this fat ass first.

C: Shut it.

INTERLUDE 5

ON SCREEN: MyRate dating app testimonial. X and Y speak to camera. Sickly sweet.

Y: Love at first site really.

X: Profile picture was super cute.

Y: Yours made me giggle.

X: That pose.

Y: Definitely the first person who popped up in my rate bracket who I was like 'Yes. Definitely yes.'

X: We matched on, when was it? A Friday morning?

Y: I was on my tea break.

X: Guzzling chocolate probably.

Y: Ah, the good old days.

X: We're on a health programme, see.

Y: I'm high risk diabetes Type 2? Nothing tragic but /

X: Better stay on the safe side you know?

X shrugs. Y smiles unconvincingly.

SCENE 5

AARON and BEA are on top of a mountain. Six months later.

A: Wooooooooooohoooooo. Christ, look!

B: The fuck you doing? Aaron!

A: Look!

B: There's no barrier!

A: It's fine!

B: Fucksake! Just. Please!

AARON laughs. Comes back from the edge and hugs her.

Idiot.

A: 'Please stand behind the yellow line'.

B: You could've fallen off.

A: See the water? You can just see the edge. That's loch
something or other. We went out on a fishing boat once
and Dad fell in.

B: D'you think the air's thinner?

A: We're not that high.

B: What did the thingy say?

A: 1000ish?

B: Highest I've ever been.

AARON sits.

It's so beautiful.

A: Hasn't changed a bit. Everything else, but not these adamantine rocks.

B: *(Quietly.)* Adamantine.

A: Unbreakable.

B: Yeah, I know.

She doesn't. Beat. AARON puts his hands to his mouth and howls.

A: Aaaaooooooooooooo! You know Bola thinks we're at an all inclusive spa. Apparently this counts as 'high risk'.

B: Rebel.

A: Used to be able to swim in there. I remember running with Mum then us jumping in stark-bollock-naked. Freeeezing. Tiny willy.

BEA digs around in her rucksack and pulls out some snacks and a medical bag. She takes a pill and offers one to AARON.

B: Altitude tablet.

A: We're really not that high.

B: There's a chance of illness at any level.

A: That's ridiculous.

B: Better than getting the bends or something.

A: Sweetie that's diving.

B: I dunno, don't wanna risk it. Don't call me 'sweetie'.

He reluctantly takes a tablet.

Don't wanna have to deal with you being all sicky.

Pause. She looks out.

Can I tell you something a bit embarrassing?

A: More embarrassing than you pooing yourself on the cross trainer?

B: Aaron!

A: There's no one here! No, go on.

B: No!

A: No, go on, please, sorry.

B: I was just gonna say that this is the first time I've been out of England.

A: Ever?

She nods.

Well I'm thrilled to take your Highland virginity.

Kiss.

B: When we have kids they're gonna be well sporty.

A: Ha, you would have to exercise a bit first.

Pause.

B: Why did you do that?

A: What? I'm teasing, you've got a beautiful /

B: No. You said 'would'. Like, I talked in the future, and you said 'would', like in the...

A: Conditional.

B: Yeah.

Beat.

A: Sorry.

B: How would you feel if I was pregnant right now?

A: Are you?!

B: No. Well I don't think so, no, I'm not, but I mean if I was, hypothetically.

A: So in the conditional?

B: Don't be a prick.

Beat.

A: I just... I'm not sure if. We're not ready.

B: Yeah I'm not saying now! But like before, when we spoke about that stuff, it was in the future, like definitely, and now I feel like you speak about it like...

A: Conditionally.

B: Yeah. Yeah. That's all.

Beat.

A: I just sometimes I wonder if... Do you think the world really needs our offspring?

Beat.

B: Would you be saying that if I was Courtney Shrier?

A: Who?

B: 9.8 girl. She's got that TV show.

A: God, no, look, it's not about /

B: Our kids would be hot.

A: No, I was a really ugly baby actually. Really fat face. Dad used to call me blobby, had a song and everything.

Sings.

'Little blobby, my blobby...'

He pulls her towards him and jiggles her. She smiles. He spots something.

A: Finch! Look.

They watch.

You can tell by how it flies, kind of dances. See?

B: I don't wanna go home.

A: That flat won't pay for itself.

B: No.

A: If we're punching above our, you know, we can /

B: No, it's perfect. I'll take more shifts, I don't mind.

A: Longer hours.

B: We'll be fine. Wanna get one of them power showers.

AARON shuffles towards the edge of the cliff and peers over.

A: Do you reckon you'd die before you hit the ground?

B: Aaron.

A: I just mean, not a bad place for it is it? Better than the Dying Rooms. Toodalooooo with a view. This is what I'd /

B: Can you get back from the edge please.

A: It's fine.

B: Seriously, please.

AARON gives a look, and hangs a foot off.

Aaron! Please!

A: It's /

B: Please! Aaron!

A: I'm only /

She starts to panic

B: *(Shouting.)* Please just, STOP IT! STOP IT!!

He comes back from the edge.

A: Hey.

She shrugs him off and moves away, shaking.

B: Mum, she…

A: What?

B: Jumped. Off Archway Bridge. When I was sixteen. Before they put them railings up everywhere.

A: Fuck. I'm sorry. I'm so sorry. God.

Long silence. She sits.

B: I should have told you, I just.

A: Sorry.

B: No, she had a shitty time. She was very depressed. Not clinical or anything, just, um.

A: Environmental.

B: Yeah.

Beat.

Um. Basically. I had a, a little brother.

A: What?

B: Yeah. A half-brother. Jamie. He had Tay-Sachs syndrome. It's a complex…condition. From her ex's side. Anyway, he died when I was thirteen. And after he went, um. Mum kind of…

She falters. Beat.

Everything had been about him for years. In and out of hospital, washing, feeding him, tube kept getting blocked.

And she was so positive, and patient. And like…proud, too. Like she'd shout at people in the street for staring at him. But after he went it was like she had nothing to…like nothing…mattered. Look I'm sorry, I should have told you this before but /

A: It's alright, you don't have to /

B: But basically she was better gone. In the nicest way, she really was.

Beat.

Never felt that people really took it seriously coz it was just…inside her, if you know what I mean.

He nods.

Not hereditary though, I promise, I'm clean /

A: Look, you don't have to… I love you. As you are. As you come.

Beat.

Pooey cross trainer and all.

She laughs. Hits him. Holds him.

B: That's why when you talk about your summer holidays or whatever, they sound fuckin' lovely, but I never, you know, I can't really… I'm not asking for sympathy.

A: I know.

B: No point mourning something I never had. Like the swimming. Can't even swim.

Pause.

A: It's weird you know, sometimes I wish I didn't have those memories at all.

B: What?

A: Well it's sad, isn't it. Nostalgia. When I think about me and Mum splashing about down there.

B: Do you miss her?

He nods. Pause.

A: 'I hold it true, whatever befall, I feel it when I sorrow most, 'tis better to have loved and lost, than never to have loved at all.' Right?

B: Maybe.

They both stare into the distance.

INTERLUDE 6

ON SCREEN: Courtney Shreir's chat show. The vibe is cheap and seedy.

HOST: Wassup guys, I'm Courtney Shrier, thank you all for clicking in. Today I'm joined by Sam Manuel, international life coach, medical miracle, and author of best-selling zine 'Up-Rate – Weird Old Tricks to Up Your Rating'. So, my viewers will be dying to ask: did you really go from 5.9 to 8.4 in two years?

INTERVIEWEE: Yes Courtney, I did.

HOST: Wow. Just wow. And the zine has been a huge success, how does that feel?

INTERVIEWEE: Yeah, incredible.

HOST: Amazing to bring hope to so many people.

INTERVIEWEE: My subscribers are optimists. Fulfilling their dreams is what gets me up in the morning.

HOST: So we all know about epigenetics and watching our micros and fit-goals, but can you give us some insight into what your courses offer?

INTERVIEWEE: Oops, that would be telling Courtney.

HOST: Not even a sneak peek?

Turns to camera.

INTERVIEWEE: Potential up-raters can sign up for a discounted introductory offer and see how they can up their rating, for a healthier future, by visiting 'weird old tricks to up your rating dot com.'

SCENE 6

AARON and BEA's new, fancier flat. Two years later. CHAR and BEA hug in the doorway. CHAR wears a huge rucksack.

B: Oh my /

C: Sorry, I probably stink, I'm /

B: Come in /

C: Filthy, I just. Fuccckin' hell, this is nice!

B: Yeah I know right.

C: Wow /

B: Have you literally just /

C: Couple of hours ago, yeah. Look a your face! Sorry bit out the blue, I just realised I had nowhere to, you know, and I wanted to see you!

B: No, it's fine.

C: Can I sit here? Sorry, I'm a bit… This place is…

She whistles. She sits. Beat.

B: So…how was it?

C: It was really amazing. Honestly Bea, I don't know where to start, it was fucking… It was so… It's like I haven't stopped for months and months, just like bang bang bang going, like yeah.

B: But what, I don't understand, what were you actually doing?

C: Can I take my shoes off?

B: Sure.

C: So I, basically I started off with that group I was telling you about, and we set off on our bikes /

B: Raising money?

C: Awareness.

B: Course.

C: Yeah and it was one of those things where one thing kind of led to another. We met this amazing grassroots group out in Serbia and stayed there for a bit, they do all this incredible social inclusion work. And it ended up turning into a kind of anti-discrimination tour.

B: Right.

C: Honestly, it was just so inspiring.

B: Sounds it.

C: And then coming back here I was like God this place is so depressing.

B: What happened to your phone?

C: Broke. And I was gonna get another one, then I just decided fuck it, you know, why do I need it?

Beat. BEA smiles.

And how are *you*? I mean what the fuck is this place eh? It's beautiful!

B: Ha, thanks, yeah, this is where I live, ha.

C: What's that?

She points to a tree.

B: Bonzai.

C: Is it supposed to be that small?

B: Yeah that's the whole point, you trim it. Prune it. It's Japanese. Aaron hates it, I think it's cute.

C: And how is he? The man. You good?

B: Yeah, really good thanks. Great actually, yeah.

Beat.

You look different.

C: So do you.

B: Do I? Old and stressed?

C: No, just different.

Beat.

B: How's the er…

C: Huntingdon's? You can say it, it's not contagious.

B: Sorry.

C: Couple of shakes, nothing major.

B: Did you look into the editing thing I sent? The stuff they're starting to do is amazing /

C: Yeah, no…

B: If there's a chance /

C: There isn't. I thought about applying for a trial but once I declare myself that's it. It's not worth it. And I don't want to anyway. This is what I am, you know, I don't know how I feel about fucking around with… I mean I cycled halfway across the world on it, I can't be too shabby.

BEA smiles. Beat. She puts on some music. Beat.

I'm guessing you're still…dealing then?

BEA nods.

Looks like it's going well.

B: Um, yeah.

C: Yeah?

B: Well there's just been a huge crack down. Have to have three nurses sign off on each test. No more swaps.

C: Right, so.

B: So one of the docs has hooked me up with...basically I've moved to blood bank work. Most people are go for the dopes now, you know the full-body /

C: Transfusions. Yeah I've heard of them. That's pretty big stuff.

B: Yeah, well it's all tightened up, so.

C: Why don't you just /

B: Yeah, no I will. Soon. Got a little savings account, once I got enough for the building work I'll /

Keys in the door. BEA jumps. AARON enters and does a double take.

A: Oh, hello ello.

B: There you are.

C: Hello monsieur!

A: What a surprise!

C: I stink, sorry.

A: Had no idea you were /

B: This one got in touch this afternoon saying she was back in town so.

C: How you doing?

A: Good, yeah, great.

B: Where've you been? It's late.

A: Well, I didn't know you'd be in, went to watch the match.

C: Oh yeah, who won?

A: *We* did, obviously! You think I'd be this happy if we didn't? No, two-nil, so back to the semi-final, down to Wembley, hey hey /

C: Nice.

A: The stars have aligned, the clouds have lifted, the future is bright and all is HEAVENLY.

B: You are so happy, look at you!

A: Course I am, course I am, everyone thought we were going to lose didn't they?

B: Congratulations.

A: Can I offer either of you ladies quelque chose à boire?

B: What?

A: Un petit bonnet de nuit?

B: Literally no idea what /

C: Dépend de ce que vous offrez?

B: What's that mean?

A: Whisky. Finest scotch.

He pulls a bottle of whisky out.

B: Where did you get that from?

A: Little victory purchase. Jura's best.

B: Jura?

A: *(To CHAR.)* Mummy's got the purse strings…

(To both.) Any takers?

C: Yeah go on then.

He kneels before BEA.

A: What about you, mon petit amour, lumière de ma vie, soutien de famille?

C: Don't let Bea on the whisky, you remember when you came up to visit me in freshers?

B: No, Char, don't /

C: Bea must've had like half a bottle /

B: Char!

C: She disappeared and we found her naked in a fountain.

B: Oh my Godddd, don't!

A: Oh so you do have a wild side!

B: Only with this biatch.

A: We should get you two out more often.

He proffers the bottle.

B: Nah I'm good.

He hands it to CHAR.

A: You know what, I'm going to um...slip into something a little more comfortable... Or as the Americans say... 'Let me go freshen up.'

He blows a kiss and exits to bedroom.

C: Oh my gosh, he's much more fun when he's high.

B: What?

C: He's great.

B: He doesn't smoke.

C: Couldn't you smell it?

B: He's not high.

C: He smelt like a fucking festival.

B: He doesn't smoke. He's just had a couple of drinks.

C: OK.

B: No, seriously, he doesn't. Probably just his stupid course friends.

C: He's still training?

B: Yeah, never ends.

C: Big bucks and white wig eventually though, no?

B: That's the plan, yeah.

> *Beat.*

C: You've lost weight you know.

B: Have I? Probably lost hair as well.

C: No, you look good.

B: Cheers. Been watching my micros innit, got a new app.

> *CHAR watches her.*

> What?

C: You haven't had a cheeky edit have you? The lipid one, the celeb thing?

B: Don't be stupid.

C: You sure?

> *CHAR pinches her.*

B: Oh my God! I've been going to the gym! Stop it! Stop it!

> *They giggle. AARON enters.*

A: Fresh as a daisy.

> *He drinks.*

> So you were off saving the world right? Any luck?

C: Yeah. Done. Finished. Nailed it.

A: Excellent. Someone's got to.

AARON sits beside BEA.

C: Awh you two are looking gooood, like something out of a catalogue.

A: Ha.

C: How comes you moved? I mean this place is /

B: Needed a bit more space.

C: Yeah?

B: Yeah. You know, just in case.

C: In case what?

B: In case we, you know.

C: What?

B: We…

A: She means in case we procreate.

Beat. CHAR looks taken aback.

C: Oh. Well I guess it's about the right… Fuck, I didn't realise you were…are you /

A: We're not.

B: Not yet.

C: Well you could fit the whole Von Trapp family in here.

A: Ha, don't know about the Von Trapps but yeah.

B: Aaron needs a bit of convincing, but we'll get there soon eh?

A: If soon means like five ten years maybe.

C: Don't you like kids?

A: No I love them, I'm just not sure I…

C: Well, two healthy people, good jobs /

A: Yeah but the world isn't healthy is it? I don't want to add to the problem.

B: We're not adding to a problem.

C: What do you mean the world isn't healthy?

A: Wait, why are we even talking about this?

C: Unhealthy in what way?

A: Well, look at it, it's /

C: I don't see any unhealthiness in here.

A: I never said there /

C: Well what do you mean then?

A: Why don't we just get a dog. A nice little rescue puppy.

B: What's the point in that?

A: Well what's the point in kids?

B: The world doesn't need more useless little mangy mongrel puppies.

A: Well the world doesn't need any more useless little…

C: What? Finish your sentence.

A: I just /

C: Bea's well above average you know, she's not /

B: Char.

A: I'm not talking about the fucking numbers or /

C: Well clearly you are.

A: I'm not a ratist! I couldn't give a shit about /

C: Well it doesn't sound like you don't.

A: Can you stop interrogating me please?

C: Why's this an issue?

A: It's not an issue! I'm not saying never, I'm not saying anything, I just, I don't know how I feel about it OK? Stop attacking me. If you want a baby go ahead, but don't put it on /

CHAR knocks over her glass/drops the bottle. Her hand shakes slightly.

C: Shit. Sorry.

B: Aaron, that's…

A: You know what, I'm just gonna…

He gets up and exits.

C: Yeah, walk away /

B: Char, please, this isn't the /

C: I think now's exactly the time if you're thinking of having a baby with this guy! What a prick!

Beat.

This is ridiculous. This is exactly what I've been /

B: But we're not on a campaign yeah, so can you just leave it. Please. Give him a minute to…

Silence.

C: Is he usually this defensive?

A: *(O.S.)* I can hear you, you know.

B: He's just in a bad mood, he's not normally like this.

A: *(O.S. shouting.)* Well, I was in a good mood….

CHAR opens mouth.

B: Can you just leave it.

Beat.

C: I hate to see you so /

B: I'm fine. We're fine. Great. Honestly.

INTERLUDE 7

AUDIO: Radio interview with MINISTER OF STATE (à la BBC Radio 4).

MINISTER: / as I've said, this is not a government scheme, and as such we cannot take responsibility. No one is forcing anyone to disclose this information.

INTERVIEWER: But it is used in A&E?

MINISTER: Well, it helps staff to prioritise to give the best level of care.

INTERVIEWER: It was an economist who popularised the nought to ten rating model was it not?

MINISTER: I believe so.

INTERVIEWER: And combining every genetic trait, from disease to behaviour, do you think that all these characteristics can be processed into one simple ranking?

MINISTER: Ha ha, it's not a 'ranking'. Anyone knows that if you want real information you have to read the breakdown. Else it's a bit like just reading the stars on a review and not the review itself, you know?

Tiny beat.

INTERVIEWER: What are your thoughts on test-upon-entry schemes at immigration points?

MINISTER: I'm not able to comment on /

SCENE 7

Outside the hospital. A few months later. Night. BEA waits. She's hunched over, cold and exhausted. DAVID enters behind her quietly. Watches her for a moment.

D: Stars are out.

She jumps.

B: Oh God you scared the shit out of me.

D: Sorry.

Beat. He sits, pulls a little pouch out of his pocket and starts to roll a spliff. She watches him.

Want some?

She makes a 'hell no' face and shakes her head.

Careful, the wind might change and you'll be stuck like that.

Beat. He carries on rolling.

Just a treat. One a day won't kill me.

B: It might.

He shrugs. BEA shivers. Looks up the road, worried.

D: You alright?

She nods.

Waiting for Dr. Salt?

She looks at him.

S'alright.

He zips his lips. Winks.

I know the situation.

B: Yeah, I know you know, else I wouldn't be so calm about it would I?

Beat.

Sorry. Sorry, I'm just. Really tired.

D: You OK?

She nods. She's not. She looks like she might cry.

Penny for your thoughts /

B: Look I'm just a bit stressed, ok.

D: OK. Sure I can't tempt you...

B: It's really bad for you.

D: So is stress.

She smiles. Sighs.

B: Um. Basically I er. I fucked up one of the orders. Nearly cost us...a lot. People already doped up with high stuff, couldn't find their names to fast-track for testing. Dr. Salt went ballistic. Managed to sort it but we've got a load more to do tonight. It's just. I'm just...tired.

He nods. Lights his spliff.

How much does she, Salt, how much does she pay you to, you know...

She mimics his lip-zip.

D: Got my nephew onto an editing trial. Pancreatic cancer. He got the all clear a few months ago.

B: That's it?

D: That's what I wanted.

B: No I don't mean, I mean congrats for him, that's great, but. You could get a decent /

D: I don't want more money.

B: Or a cheeky rate raise.

D: I don't want /

B: Could help with life insurance.

D: I'm 9.1. Fit as a fiddle. But thanks.

B: You're 9.1?!

He nods.

9. /

D: Yes.

B: Pffff why you doing this then?

D: Why not?

B: I... I dunno.

He takes a drag. Exhales. She wafts the smoke away from her. Beat.

Did you go uni?

He nods. Takes a drag.

D: Went straight into finance. Hated it. Did army training. Hated it. Did teaching, loved it, but knackering, and system's a mess. Was volunteering on the psychiatric ward here, and saw a vacancy for porter, and thought, 'Door-keeping. Care-taking. Keeping the door. Taking care. That sounds nice'. Twenty years later, here I am.

B: Mad.

D: Not really. Happiest I've been.

B: What coz you watch the poor, sick low-raters crawling in and out and feel really great about yourself? Hang around the loonies on the psyche ward and think thank fuck that's not me?

Beat. He frowns.

D: No. I talk to the patients, check in with staff, maintain the building, do what needs doing...and then I lock up, have a smoke, and roll on home to cook dinner for my wife. And I feel...good.

Pause. She watches him smoke.

B: So I'm supervisor now yeah /

D: I know, congratulations /

B: No, I mean yeah, thanks, but I mean I test a lot of people right, and I do the whole thing now, and I always look at people first right and try to guess, like predict, and it's basically impossible. It's amazing. I love it, that moment just before the numbers crunch, when no one knows, and then it drops in. 9.1. Ha.

Beat.

What's your wife?

D: A teacher.

B: No, like…

D: Oh. Um…five point something. Alzheimer's.

B: Sorry.

D: Well it hasn't really started yet.

Beat.

B: How long you been together?

D: Thirty…thirty-three years.

B: Wow. Where d'you meet?

D: Swimming pool.

B: Really?!

D: Yeah.

B: Like in the water?

D: Yep, you can see what you're getting yourself in can't you. No surprises.

B: Ha, well.

He frowns.

I just...

D: I know what you meant.

Beat.

B: Sorry.

Pause.

But you're happy, right?

D: Huh?

B: You said you were happy. 'The happiest'.

D: Well I don't know how quantifiable it is but... Yes.

BEA raises her eyebrows. Then looks up the road again. Shivers.
DAVID watches her in silence.

Are you happy?

She looks at him. His phone rings in his pocket. A tinkling ringtone.

Sorry.

He silences it.

B: No, take it.

D: It can wait.

Beat. BEA looks up the road.

B: I don't agree with it. Believe in it. Dealing. Cheating.
Buying privilege. Please don't think I'm... I think it's...

DAVID shrugs.

D: If there's a game people will always find a way to cheat. I'm
not an umpire, I'm a...reluctant spectator dragged along
to the sidelines. It's not my business to get involved in
anyone's business.

She nods. He watches her.

Why do you do it if you hate it so much?

B: Um. You know those houses on the East side of Dulwich Park? The tall ones.

D: Yes, beautiful.

B: Perfect. Me and Mum used to walk 'round, pretend we lived there. I want to…actually live there.

He nods. Beat.

D: I had a friend in one of those houses. God, must be… twenty years ago.

B: Yeah?

D: Mmm. Bit different back then mind, more bohemian I suppose. Henry. Henry Marett-Selva. Nice guy. Funny one. Tragic, really.

B: Oh.

D: Yeah. He was a good man Henry. A surgeon. Gentle. Very tall. Kind of elegant. It was the most beautiful house. One of those grand ones with the reddy-brown bricks. And a huge garden. You don't see many like that now. Huge, and messy, like if you closed your eyes and spun around you might never get out. Big old climbing frame. Long grass. White wooden swing-seat. Him and his wife, er… Marta. Marta Marett-Selva. They'd throw these amazing summer parties. Barbecues, with fairy lights in the trees, and music, and kids running riot, staying up way past bedtime, making mischief. They had these two little girls. Sadie and Siena. Lovely girls, jet black hair, kind of wild. I remember them dragging me down to the pond all sparkly eyes and gappy-teeth to show me the tadpoles hatching. 'Look uncle David! Look, it's come to life, look at its tail! Look at it wiggle!'

But the parties stopped because, well… Henry started gardening. Funny. He asked me for tips at first, got green fingers myself see. And there was something quite sweet about it. It was his little project and he took it all so seriously. Pruned back the bushes. And planted small things at first, beans, herbs. Did it all so carefully. Watched. Waited. But not much grew. So he turned a new patch, a bit bigger, and had some luck. I remember him bounding out like a puppy to show me his first carrots coming through. So proud. And the next time I came 'round another patch of grass had gone. And then a bit more. And then suddenly he'd churned up half the garden, ploughed it up with one of those electric things. The climbing frame went. And the swing-seat. And the kids stopped playing out. Weren't allowed. I remember one time I was 'round one of them kicked a ball and it went sailing, smack, right into the tomatoes, and Henry screamed, red face, furious, 'Have some respect! This isn't a playground!' And poor little Siena, sulked off with a big frown on her face like this. Soon he'd ploughed the whole garden up. Made these plastic walkways so he wouldn't step on the, you know, the seedlings.

And him and Marta…well things didn't… And Henry stopped going to work. Barely went out. And whenever I was over he would always be running off to fiddle with something or other, meticulously measuring, watering, all these little lines, perfect rows. It all had to be just so. But no pride anymore. No joy. I remember standing in the kitchen comforting the poor guy when his cucumbers came out wonky. This grown man, wet face, crying, inconsolable, and me saying 'I'll take them. I like them like that. They taste the same.' He wanted them like you'd get in the shops. Nothing's stuck with me quite like that look. Hollow.

Devastating. Poor guy. Poor kids. Very sad. And that garden.

Beat. BEA stares at him.

Right. I should lock up.

He yawns.

Be kind to yourself Bea Tennyson-Williams.

He gets his keys out, and makes to go.

B: What happened to him though? Your friend.

D: Oh. He died. Choked on one of his tomatoes. Got it lodged in his throat. Perfectly round. Spherical. Acted like a kind of stopper in his oesophagus.

Beat.

Too darn smooth eh. Too darn round. Too darn smooth. Too darn round.

He does his little bow and exits, leaving her in the dark staring after him.

END OF ACT ONE.

Act Two

News reportage.

REPORTER: ... I'm here outside Westbourne Farm where late last night, a joyful wedding reception turned into a nightmare party. This mixed-rate couple from Dundee were celebrating their first evening as newly-weds, when a group of pro-rate activists vandalised and set fire to several cars outside the family farm on the outskirts of Midmar, Aberdeenshire. Luckily no one was seriously hurt as a result of the attacks, but for the couple and their families, what should have been a joyful celebration certainly hasn't gone to plan. Three members of a local far-right pro-rate group are currently being held for /

SCENE 8

Tram stop. A year later. Early hours. We hear AARON and BEA from O.S.

A: *(Singing O.S.)* ...here's the good old whisky knock it down... Rolling home, rolling home, by the light of the silvery mooooooon /

B: *(O.S.)* OK OK, put me down! No! Aaron!

A: *(O.S.)* Happy shall I be with a barmaid on my knee and the /

B: *(O.S.)* Shhhh! Put me down!

AARON enters carrying BEA. AARON is drunk. BEA is barefoot, hitting AARON with her high heels.

A: Happy shall I be with a barmaid on my kneeeee and the shadow of her knockers on the wall!

He plonks her down.

B: Probably woken up the whole street you mentalist.

AARON looks at the board.

A: Delayed. We have twelve minutes. Oh hello! Did you see Char went home with Jason?

B: Yeah, was wondering which one it was gonna be.

A: Ouch.

B: No, she can do what she wants…

A: But…

B: But nothing, it's what she does.

A: Her friends are…interesting.

B: God yeah didn't expect her to bring her crusty entourage.

A: Bit intense /

B: Yeah it was a birthday party not a fucking rally.

He laughs. She glugs from a water bottle.

A: You look hot. I like your dress.

B: It's real silk. Actual silk, feel.

A: Mmmm sleek. Slippery.

B: You want some?

She offers water.

A: I say we try for a quick nightcap over there.

B: It'll be closing.

A: Just one. It's cold.

B: What time are we up tomorrow?

A: Depends what time we get to sleep…

B: You wanna lie in?

A: You got places to be?

B: Well, I said I'd be at my other husband's house for lunch so…

A: Shut it.

She passes him water.

No nightcap then?

B: You don't need it.

A: I am entirely sober and able to make my own decisions mother.

B: You'll thank me tomorrow.

A: Yeah but it's not tomorrow, it's now, so no thank you.

Beat.

B: I didn't drink anything tonight you know.

A: What? Yes you did.

B: Nah I didn't.

A: I bought you a shot.

B: Didn't have it.

A: What?

B: Gave it to some girl.

A: You gave your birthday shot to some random girl?

B: I just wanted to see if it was still fun, and it was. It's just I've been thinking maybe we should, we could, try not drinking for a bit, or, I dunno.

A: What's going on?

B: We always feel like shit the next day and ruin Sunday recovering and then suddenly it's Monday again and /

A: That's what Sunday's for!

B: You know what I mean though. You're always proper mopey. If we woke up feeling normal, we could do stuff, but instead tomorrow, I can see it already, we're gonna snooze like twenty times and then you'll spend the whole day all moody, talking about how shit work is and all the food you want but can't be bothered to go and get.

A: W-w-w-w-wait hold on.

B: It's true though, isn't it?

A: Why are we talking about this?

B: What?

A: We were having fun.

B: It's just it's basically a poison, we're basically poisoning our bodies. What's the point of minding our epigenetics if we're just gonna drink all those toxins? And you get so low on a hangover /

A: Yeah so don't talk about it now while I'm up! Gonna feel shit enough tomorrow without ruining tonight by talking about how shit I'm gonna feel tomorrow!

B: I just /

A: Nope. Nope nope Bea Bea Tennyson-Williams.

He covers her mouth with his hand.

B: *(Through his hand.)* Aaron...

A: Close your eyes.

B: *(Still through his hand...)* Aaron...

She closes her eyes. He creeps backwards.

I can hear you...

He takes a book from his pocket, creeps back and hands it to her.

What's this?

A: Look at the date. Been in the family for years.

B: It's beautiful!

A: All his poems. Well the good ones.

She kisses him. He twirls her around.

I'd do anything in the world for you BeaBea Tennyson-Williams.

B: Ah! Aaron!

A: Honestly, I'd hop up the raindrops to the clouds for you if I could...just so I could push them out the way and the sun could find you.

B: You're such a cheesy /

He covers her mouth.

A: I want to make you the happiest woman in the world.

He kisses her forehead.

From the top of your head.

He bends down.

To the tips of your...

B: You know what would make me happy?

A: What?

B: You *know*.

A: Not drinking?

B: No...

A: What?

She stares at him.

OK.

B: What?

A: OK, let's make a baby.

B: Really?!

A: Yeah, fuck it!

B: Really really?

A: Yes!

B: Oh my God!

A: *(Singing, loudly.)* Happy birthday to Beeeaaaa, Happy Birthday to Beeeaaaa…

B: Sshhhhhhhhh!

She squeezes him.

A: One condition.

B: No, you can't add a / !

A: Come home earlier.

B: Love, I have to /

A: I'm being serious.

B: OK. OK, I'll try.

Beat. They both smile.

A: Better get working on it then eh?

She laughs.

B: Let's get a taxi!

A: Yeah fuck it!

He carries her O.S., bouncing.

Singing.

Happy shall I be with a Beeeeeaaa on my kneee and the shadow of her /

INTERLUDE 9

ON SCREEN: Advert: 'The Thring Group'. A well-dressed rep walks through public school grounds, talking to camera emphatically.

SPEAKER: We at The Thring Group believe that every child deserves the best chance of success.

When children show signs of faltering concentration in early years, many parents look ahead with trepidation at academic struggle, failed entry tests, and bleak employment prospects. They see a clear division between those who will strive, and those who will *thrive*.

But this doesn't have to be the case. We offer personalised CRISPR editing therapy for genes associated with the autistic spectrum. We watch children move from the bottom to the top set practically overnight. We help to *write* success into the future of your child.

Book in for a consultation today.

SCENE 9

AARON and BEA's flat. Six months later.

A: *Please* don't make me feel like I'm being /

B: I told you, I had a late shift.

A: 'til eleven?

Beat.

B: What?

AARON stares at her.

A: I called in. They said you left clinic at eight.

Pause.

They said you left with Dr. Salt.

B: Right so you're going detective on me now?

A: Please just be honest with me.

B: What?

A: Please...just be /

B: What? If you're suggesting something do you wanna just spit it out?

A: Well what do you want me to / say

B: Are you actually suggesting that I'm... What?

A: Well?

B: Say it.

A: God don't make me feel like I'm going mad! I'm not being... I'm not...

B: You actually think that I /

A: Well what am I supposed to...what's going on?!

B: Dr. Salt is a woman!

Beat.

A: What?

Pause.

B: Fuck. I'm dealing.

Beat.

A: What?

B: Fuck. Blood. I'm dealing blood. Fuck.

A: So you're not...

B: No.

A: And Dr /

B: She knows people. Hooks me up.

Pause.

A: So you help people fake their /

B: Yeah.

A: Jesus.

B: But I don't actually do much. Salt, she does all the actual…she does the proper stuff, the dopes, and the… the schmoozing. She's posh, well-connected. I barely do anything really, I just help source the right blood, and fast-track them for testing… I don't /

A: Right.

B: But I don't believe in it. I don't support it, I don't, I promise.

A: You don't support it.

B: No! Of course I don't.

A: Well what do you do it for then?!

B: What the fuck do you think I do it for Aaron?

A: I'll be earning properly soon.

B: I know that, but I just wanted to give us a bit of /

A: It's dangerous.

B: I'm careful.

A: No. No, you're stupid! You're fucking /

B: I'm not stu /

A: If you get caught we'd lose our jobs, I'd be struck off, you'd go to… I'd lose my entire /

B: Yes, but /

A: You have to stop.

B: I will. I've got a target, then /

A: No you need to stop. Now.

Pause.

B: I'm sorry.

A: Why didn't you tell me?

B: I didn't want you to think I was...

Beat.

Mum didn't leave me savings. She left me debts. Big ones. I don't come from anything Aaron, you know that, but you don't know how shit it was, quite how bleak, coz I've never...but it was, it was bleak. I just want things to be good. I mean I'm doing it for us, I'm saving, so we can have a nice, a good /

A: God I don't need any of this, fucking cotton sheets, fucking pineapples.

B: No?

A: No.

B: No?

A: No!

B: Well maybe I do, maybe I deserve it.

Beat.

I was gonna stop, before, but was thinking when the baby comes it'd be /

A: We don't have a /

B: Yeah but when we do, it'll be good to have some security right?

A: I never see you. What's the point of having cash if I never see you.

Pause.

B: OK, I'll stop. I promise. I'll stop. Promise. Sorry.

Beat. AARON stares at the floor.

I understand why you're angry.

He shakes his head.

A: I'm relieved.

Long pause.

All that shit. All that... That's not us, OK. We're us. Here, now. This is what matters. This.

He holds her head.

This. Your face. The rest of the world doesn't exist.

BEA nods. Pause.

B: I. I've missed my period.

A: What?

INTERLUDE 10

City street. Distant sounds of sirens and glass smashing. Blurry/muffled footage of people walking down dark street, barely visible. Voices off-screen:

RIOTER 1: Few things of meds. Creams. Syringes. Sell them innit.

RIOTER 2 jumps into wheelchair.

RIOTER 2: Fam this is siccckk.

RIOTER 3: Nah don't, you'll break it, my son /

RIOTER 1: You crack me up man.

RIOTER 3: Here, let me say some /

RIOTER 1: Fam /

RIOTER 3: No, let me say this, yeah, send this out.

Then RIOTER 3's face appears more clearly on screen, close up.

No seriously, this wheelchair's for my son, no seriously. I've come back FOUR TIMES asking. They keep changing the forms, allowances keep getting less. I queued eight hours last week. Eight hours. Then some cunt comes and tells me they ain't got one for him, they need to give high-rate cases priority with the wheelchairs. It's bullsh /

SCENE 10

A casino. A couple of months later. The sounds of onscreen betting. AARON sits staring darkly at a screen. CHAR enters. She comes up behind him quietly.

C: What've you got your money on?

A: Red.

C: How come?

A: Why not.

C: Does your wife know you gamble?

AARON turns quickly and recognises her. CHAR chuckles.

A: What are you doing here?

C: What are *you* doing here?

Beat.

S'alright, I won't tell. Have seen a few city boys here actually. Mainly bankers and stockbrokers though. As if they didn't get it out their systems in the office.

A: You're not a gambler.

C: How d'you know?

A: I've never seen you in here before.

C: I've seen you.

A: Right, bit creepy.

Beat.

Have you really?

She nods.

You haven't told Bea?

She shakes head.

She just wouldn't like it if I was, you know. I never put down that much money I just. Why you hanging around here anyway?

C: The charity I run supports people ostracised by rate culture. We do integration support, counselling, advocacy. Statistics say casinos are a popular hangout. Scooped up a few subs here last month. Spotted you.

A: I'm not low-rate.

C: Didn't say you were.

A: And I'm not ostracised. I'm doing my pupillage. In the city.

C: I know.

He looks back at the screen.

We help people remember their self-worth. The past and the present are hard enough to deal with. The future's a whole different ball game.

A: Ha, so you're like a missionary. Wading through the depths of London's underworld to save our souls.

C: Well your soul doesn't need saving.

She smiles. AARON stares intently at the screen.

Spotted you a few times. Been waiting for the right moment to say hello.

Beat.

I don't think there's anything wrong with enjoying a bit of risk, Aaron. A middle-finger up at inevitability.

She sits down next to him. Beat.

When everything seems so planned out, it's OK to want to indulge in a bit of chance. A bit of undetermined thrill. I get that.

Beat.

You're struggling, aren't you.

Beat. He nods.

He looks up at her.

It's human. We're not perfect. None of us are. We're not supposed to be. We don't work like that.

Long pause.

A: *(Quietly.)* I don't know if I can keep it up anymore.

C: You shouldn't have to.

She reaches out and touches him.

A: What are you trying to do?

INTERLUDE 11

SCREEN: Courts of Justice. DR. DEVKI SALT walks briskly, accompanied by security. Several microphones and cameras are thrust in her direction. She looks exhausted but triumphant.

SALT: ...this has been a witch hunt of epic proportions. But I am happy to report that I have been acquitted of all charges relating to genetic fraud and of all accusations of my being involved in the non-consensual sourcing of high-rate blood. I am pleased to declare that I have been found innocent on all accounts, and I thank my lawyers and the jury for their unwavering support, and hope we can all move /

SCENE 11

AARON and BEA's flat. A few months later. BEA sits with a book.
AARON has just entered.

B: No one!

A: I thought I heard…

B: What?

A: I thought I… Doesn't matter.

   Beat. BEA laughs.

B: I'm messing with you! I was reading to bump.

A: What?

B: Sorry.

A: Fuck, I thought I was going… That's not funny!

B: Sorry! Sorry, your face, sorry, I was just. Apparently it's
good for language development?

A: You fucker!

B: Shhhhh!

   BEA covers her tummy in faux alarm. AARON puts his mouth to it.

A: Come in baby, I repeat, come in baby. This is your daddy
speaking. Don't listen to your mother, she's an evil cow,
and /

B: Oi.

   BEA hits him over the head with the book. He grabs it. Clears throat.

A: 'The seasons bring the flower again, And bring the firstling
to the flock, And in the dusk of thee, the clock, Beats out
the little lives of men'… Christ do you want the poor sod
to hang itself with its umbilical chord?

B: You gave it to me. Anyway, they can't actually hear, it's just
aural stimulation.

A: Oral stimulation eh?

She laughs. He leans in.

B: Have you been smoking?

A: I. Had one.

B: Aaron!

A: Sorry.

The moment is lost. They move away from each other. Pause.

A: How was work?

B: Fine, you?

He shrugs.

A: The Dr. Salt thing's all over the news.

BEA nods.

The accused walks free.

BEA nods.

She's a savvy woman. Those legal fees must have been…

Whistle. BEA nods.

You're lucky you got out when you /

B: Yeah, I know.

A: If you'd still /

B: I'd rather not talk about it.

A: Yeah well me neither.

Pause.

B: Saw Char on the way home.

A: Oh yeah?

B: She asked after you.

A: Yeah?

Beat.

Did you tell her…?

B: Er no, not yet. I should. I will, I just… It's awkward isn't it, she was always the one that planned stuff, named her kids. I mean we both did actually, we had these drawings, stupid cartoon pictures of how it would all be /

A: Did you draw me?

B: Oh yeah. Every last bit of you… Ha. But no, she like properly planned, picked names, dresses, planned it all out, and I sometimes feel…

A: You shouldn't.

B: I know.

A: It's not your fault.

B: She's been weird lately.

A: Weird how?

B: I dunno, just weird.

A: What she's going through must be /

B: Yeah.

A: Maybe she's jealous.

B: Yeah. I dunno.

A: Well, wait 'til you're ready. What she doesn't know won't hurt her.

B: S'pose.

Long pause.

A: I. I'd like to talk to you about something.

B: OK…?

Pause.

A: Um.

Beat.

Um. My dad's um… He's around tomorrow, and I was thinking. I was wondering if we'd like to ask him over.

B: Your dad?

A: Yeah, thought he could see the place. Meet you and bump.

B: Tomorrow?

A: Thought we could have lunch.

B: What the fuck Aaron?

A: You've always said you want to meet him, I'd really like you to, and I thought /

B: Tomorrow?!

A: Well, yeah.

B: I…Why? This is a bit… I mean, what?

A: Well I just thought, he's passing through.

B: But. I need some warning I /

A: Are you busy?

B: No! No, it's just I need to clean up, sort the place out. Myself out. Is he expecting to eat?

A: Well I imagined we could but /

B: The floor's dirty.

A: It doesn't matter.

B: I'll have to buy some /

A: Let's just eat out.

B: What does he like?

A: We can eat out.

B: No I. No.

A: What?

B: Sorry. I don't want to, er, sorry. You just go meet him. Bit of warning and we'll have him over next time yeah?

Pause.

A: OK.

B: Sorry.

A: No. Sorry.

Pause. AARON stares into space. Exhales.

B: Been looking at schools.

A: Yeah?

B: Nightmare.

A: Bit soon isn't it?

B: Tina put hers down before she was even pregnant.

A: Woah, what?

B: We'll probably have to look at evening tuition too.

A: Well, cross that bridge when we, you know. They'll have your brains anyway.

B: I'm not actually that clever, I just work hard. What IQ rating did you get? In the breakdown? We might be OK.

A: Can't remember.

B: Wanna check? I brought my thing home.

She pulls machine out of bag.

A: Is that allowed?

B: Wanted to check mine off-grid. It's the new model, super fast.

A: God, don't bring that home, it's creepy.

B: Sorry.

> *Beat.*

A: Sorry. I'm really tired.

B: You ill?

A: Tired.

B: There's a new flu strain going around.

> *BEA pulls a face mask out of her bag.*

A: I'm not ill! I'm fine.

B: You don't seem fine.

A: It's just.

B: What?

A: I... It's just this time of year. Heavy. I hate waking up every morning in the dark.

B: We should get those daylight emitters.

A: I think I need...

B: What?

A: I don't know. I thought, if you wanted. Do you want to go on holiday?

B: What?

A: We could go to the countryside? Have a break? It's just the hours right now, it's like it never stops. And however early I get in, people are always there earlier, and stay later, and work quicker. Like... I don't know how they do it. And I'm sure they're giving me extra work because sometimes I come back to my desk after lunch and there's actually more stuff, someone's added stuff? It kind of feels like giving in if I take days off, but if you wanted, I think I'd like to, you know, and we should make the most of having the two of us /

B: Hey.

A: Please don't think I'm... I'm not weak, I'm just. I'm so tired.

B: Hey. Come here. Course you're not weak.

He goes to kiss her. She turns her head and pulls the mask on.

A: I'M NOT ILL!

Long silence.

I'm sorry I'm. I'm just exhausted. Sorry.

B: It's alright. So am I.

Pause. AARON moves towards the door.

Oh I forgot, someone called for you from the sperm bank. Asked if you want to donate some jizz.

A: Oh right.

B: They'll keep bugging. They love city boys.

A: Yeah, just can't get the time off.

B: I reckon they should let you. It should be like social responsibility. Like jury duty. Cum duty.

AARON smiles.

A: In-cum tax.

BEA chuckles.

Who knew mine would be so coveted.

B: 'Lord Tennyson's coveted cum'. A young wife's lament.

AARON laughs.

Sure we can spare a…

She makes a jerking gesture. AARON chuckles.

A: What's this?

B: *(Guiltily.)* A mango…

A: No…

B: It just looked so juicy.

A: Naughty.

He approaches slowly, and she lets him kiss her. Beat. He exits to bathroom. Sound of tap running and him drinking.

B: Don't drink the tap water!

A: I'm not!

B: *(Running O.S. after him.)* You are, I can hear you! It's not worth /

INTERLUDE 12

AUDIO or SCREEN: Evening news.

NEWS REPORTER: … Mr Thomas Obaju, well-known for having a rating of exactly 9.84, the highest on record in the UK, has been murdered. He was reported missing on Tuesday night after leaving his gym in East London and the remains of his corpse were found by a canal in Maida Vale this morning with several puncture wounds and syringe insertions. A statement from the police describes his death as 'sad and futile'. It is not clear whether his murder was a political statement or merely another blood theft, but the authorities believe it to be a combination of the two. Despite the introduction of the international DNA database, reports of blood crimes such as these are still on the rise. The police recommend that any known high-raters consider extra security, and any suspicious behaviour or information regarding illegal blood activity should be reported immediately /

SCENE 12

Hospital consultation booth. Three months later. BEA now has a proper bump. CHAR has just entered. Very occasionally, she is shaky in her movement.

B: Twenty-six weeks?

C: Wow. That's. Wow.

B: You OK?

C: Yeah. Congratulations. It suits you.

B: Thanks.

    Beat.

C: And is everything OK?

B: Yeah.

C: Yeah?

B: Yeah, great.

C: I just thought…

B: What?

C: Well you didn't tell me, why didn't you /

B: Wanted to wait for the right, didn't want to do it on the /

C: Oh.

B: Sorry.

C: I've tried to call a few times, been worried /

B: No, sorry, I've been so busy. It's all been mad. Work and…

    Beat. CHAR reaches out and touches BEA's belly shakily. Silence.

How's your…

    CHAR shrugs. Pause.

C: I'm going to go to America.

B: Oh yeah?

C: The movements growing over there. I've been asked to go
and head up a campaign.

B: Wow, that's cool.

C: Yeah. But basically, the reason I came actually is, well they
test on entry don't they so I'll need a transfusion /

B: Sshhh! Are you mad?!

C: *(Whispering.)* I'll need it soon. I'll need it right before I fly,
it's /

B: You can't bring this here.

C: Now you're high up /

B: Sshh! Look, I gave up. I'm out. Sorry.

C: But you were helping /

B: No, I wasn't /

C: You were.

B: No I wasn't! The only ones I 'helped' were rich Char, it's a
business, it's not some revolution.

C: But I couldn't have done anything I've done /

B: Do you really think you masquerading as high-rate is
helping the /

C: Yes, coz I'm more useful if people think I'm... We need
people on the inside who can /

B: No. No, listen. If this is the reason you're here then please
leave. I can't help OK? Sorry.

C: Ratism's worse over there, you must've seen it! It's *their*
model. If we can crack *them* then we can... Look if
I've only got a few years then I have to... I have to do
something, make some kind of /

B: So this is about your legacy then?

C: No, it's... It's all about education, seeing behind the numbers. That's what the campaign does. It asks for government responsibility, confidentiality. Fights prejudice. Questions how social worth can be ranked one to ten. Or why autism is rated the same as heart disease. Depression as diabetes. How being predisposed to rule-breaking is on par with breast cancer, it's political.

B: It won't make any difference.

C: It's political!

B: I'm not gonna stand here and let you preach at /

C: Bea, please, this is a moral /

B: *(Whispering)* Do you know where the high-blood comes from? For the doping? It's not all free range.

C: It's worth it.

B: Who the fuck do you think you are? Robin Hood?

C: There are people over there lobbying for forced sterilisation of low-raters!

B: Well depending on the particular breakdowns that might be the right thing to do.

Beat.

C: What?

B: In the long-term hereditary stuff will be phased out won't it, and it's horrible, but it'll get better.

C: What?

B: The world doesn't need more low-rate offspring Char. Maybe it's about investing in our future.

C: You sound like the press.

B: I'm just saying that maybe /

C: I know what you're saying.

B: I spent six years watching my brother die from a genetic deformity and then my mum go fucking mental. All I'm saying is, if her boyfriend had been tested then it wouldn't've... I'm just saying, maybe there'll be some benefits.

Beat.

C: Did you love him? Your brother.

B: Of course I did.

Beat.

I also loved my mum.

Pause.

C: Where's all this ratist bullshit coming from?

B: I'm not /

D: *(O.S.)* Knock knocckkk.

DAVID sticks his head in.

I have a delivery for you.

AARON enters, looks at CHAR in surprise. DAVID does his bow and exits.

A: Oh. Hi. I was waiting out...hi.

C: Not at work?

B: Taken the day off.

A: A bit of R&R.

B: We're going out for lunch.

C: Oh. How romantic. Didn't know you got this one up the duff. Bit of a shock eh. Congrats.

A: Thanks.

Beat.

B: Char's been offered a job in America.

A: What? Wow, amazing!

C: Thanks. So what flavour is it?

A: Sorry?

C: Boy or girl?

A: Oh /

B: / Oh. Ha, we're keeping it a surprise.

A: More exciting that way.

C: Retro.

She smiles. Beat.

B: Why don't you go wait in the reception love, we were just having a /

A: Oh yes, I'll er. Nice to see you.

He looks CHAR in the eye as he exits. BEA catches it. Silence. CHAR stares at BEA.

C: Bea /

B: No, look. Listen. Things are good for me now OK, really good, I'm getting my shit together, so please don't come here messing things up, criticising me, or eyeing up Aaron or whatever the fuck you're doing, or making me feel guilty about not wanting to throw myself in front of every fucking news camera with a placard about stuff we can't do anything about. I'm not interested.

Beat.

I'm sorry things are shit for you. I really am.

Pause. Tentatively, CHAR reaches out to touch her.

C: Is everything alright?

B: Yes, fine. Great.

C: Yeah?

B: Yeah. So just try to be happy for me OK?

Beat.

C: OK.

Silence.

(Whispering.) Please sort me a fast-track at the eight-plus bank. Please.

Beat. BEA shakes her head.

B: You'll have to find someone else. Sorry. I'm sticking to phlebotomy. Clean.

CHAR scoffs.

Legal.

C: It must be like Russian roulette, waiting for the numbers to appear and watching their faces.

B: Not really. Most of the time it's newborns now so.

C: It's just their parents' faces then.

B: They normally have a pretty good idea beforehand.

C: There are anomalies though.

B: Of course.

C: And then what do you do.

B: I give them their rights and hand over.

C: And how long do they usually keep it?

B: It depends. People often don't take subs home at all. It's easier. Good luck with the job.

CHAR goes to leave. She turns as if to speak.

What?

C: Doesn't matter.

INTERLUDE 13

ON SCREEN: Campaign video. Inspirational backing music.

ONE: When we found out we were going to have a baby it was a dream come true.

TWO: Al cried.

ONE: I did.

TWO: Our financial situation meant that in-vitro wasn't possible; so when the test was positive and the embryo healthy it felt like a, well...

ONE: A miracle.

TWO: But when she was born prematurely, blind and with a rating of 2.8 it came as a bit of a shock. We didn't think we'd have the finances or time to support her and her needs.

ONE: We were very worried.

TWO: It was awful.

ONE: We didn't realise how much DNA methylation happens in the last trimester and in the weeks after birth. Things can change so dramatically.

TWO: But thanks to lobby groups like CPNT we were able to work out what options were available to us and know our rights.

ONE: The legalisation of post-natal abortion has completely changed our lives. A year later we had another girl who was born at 6.1. Charlotte is now in year 1 and thriving.

TWO: She's an angel.

ONE: It's down to the work of people such as CPNT that we were able to have the child of our dreams and give her the life she deserves.

TWO: So we encourage everyone to:

ONE and TWO: Know your rights.

Big smiles.

VOICEOVER: Foetuses falling below 3.1 may be aborted within the first twenty-eight days after birth. Current law does not allow termination after this point. Check your local health centre or online portal for more information.

SCENE 13

Flat. A month later. BEA's bump is bigger. She prunes the bonzai nervously. She waits.

Keys in door. AARON enters.

A: Alright Bea-Bea.

B: You left your phone at home.

A: I know. Moron. God it's freezing out there. You OK?

Beat.

B: What's Milbury Care Home?

Beat. AARON's face drops.

A: What?

B: Someone from Milbury Care Home called.

A: Why, what's happened?

B: Why's your dad in a care home?

A: W-what did they say, is he OK?

B: His 'carer' phoned, said he's had an 'episode'? Stopped taking his meds, set fire to the bed, tried to jump out of the /

A: Fuck!

B: Why's he taking meds? Why's your Dad in a /

A: Is he OK?

B: Yeah. Yeah he's 'stable' apparently. Gonna transfer him to a high support unit. What's going on?

A: Bea /

B: Why's your father in psychiatric care?!

A: I... I have to go see /

B: AARON! WHAT THE FUCK IS GOING ON?

Beat.

A: He's. I... I didn't want to do it like /

B: Do what?

A: I...

B: DO WHAT AARON?

A: He's schizophrenic.

Beat.

I've been trying... I've been wanting to tell you, I. Fuck. Fuck!

Beat.

I have to go.

B: No.

A: I don't want to do this now, I have to /

AARON heads towards the door.

B: Don't you dare walk out the door.

A: Bea /

105

B: Wait. Sit down.

He looks at her.

Sit. Down.

He does. Silence.

How long have you known about your dad?

Beat.

A: Since I was...forever.

Beat.

B: And...and what are you then? Really?

A: I don't know.

B: Just tell me!

A: I honestly don't know! I've never wanted to, I've never been rated. I mean, I nearly did once, when I came in for a blood test, back when... But I was applying for my training and, you know, any glimmer of mental health, or anything really, in the city, there'd be no point. I couldn't have it on my file. So I. Got rid of it.

Pause.

B: The day. In the hospital?

Beat.

Pineapple Juice Day?

Aaron nods.

Right. Right. So you...

A: I didn't realise it was an opt-out scheme, they just did it, and I needed to get it back before it was tested so I... I panicked.

Beat.

B: You...

Beat.

I could have lost my job. You could've cracked my head open!

A: I'm sorry. I'm so sorry.

BEA brings her bag over and pulls out a syringe and testing device.

Please don't do this now.

B: Stay still.

A: Please don't /

B: I don't wanna hurt you, stay still. Stay still!

He relents. She extracts the blood expertly and presses a button.

Silence.

A: Bea.

B: It'll take a few minutes.

A: I don't want to /

BEA launches at him, screaming and hitting. Then breaks away, holding her belly.

B: What is in here?! What am I carrying in here?!

A: We don't know, it'll probably be fine! It'll probably be... It'll...

Silence. They wait.

The device makes a 'beep' sound. BEA looks at him. Presses a button. An electronic voice announces:

DEVICE: Two. Point. Two.

Beat. They look at the screen. BEA presses it again.

Two. Point. Two.

A: I.

BEA reads in disbelief.

Oh God.

Long silence.

So I am, I do have…?

She nods. Silence.

B: You're a cocktail of crap.

Long pause.

A: I thought he was having a good patch. Moved him from hospital into Milbury and it seemed to be better. I've tried to tell you. I wanted you to meet him, I've wanted to tell you, I tried, I'd decided to, see I've been seeing this counsellor and he said I should. I tried, but I just.

Beat.

I've noticed things lately. Moods. You know I've been finding things…but I hoped I was being, well. Paranoid. There's a family history. Great Aunt was manic depressive. Hung herself. Hanged.

B: It's a collection of genes, bio-markers, lots of crossover between them. Alfred Lord himself was bipolar wasn't he. Ha… Remember that from school.

Beat.

A: Look, we don't care about this stuff right?

B: But the world does! What planet are you living on? Our child could be a sub as well, do you know what that means? They'd be nothing. Couldn't do anything. They'd be /

A: But look at me! I'm as low-rate as it gets! But I'm killing it. I'm assisting one of the best barristers in the country! I've just been offered a tenancy Bea. I'm actually doing things, big stuff. They think I'm good blood so they treat me like

I am. And yeah, I won't live very old, I'll probably lose my marbles, and I might develop cancer, or be a carrier of all kinds of shit, I dunno, you tell me, it's all there, but until any of those things affect me I'm fine, I am fine.

Beat.

I always said I wasn't sure we should /

B: But we have! You put one inside me! You've watched me grow, study names, pick schools /

A: I got excited. And I hoped it would have all of our good, not just our bodies, but our good, you know, and I hoped it, he or she, might be OK, I might be OK, we might be lucky.

B: Science isn't about luck. Life isn't about luck.

Pause.

Did Char know about this?

A: She's been very supportive. She sorted out the counsellor. She's been trying to make me to tell you. She was very angry when she found out you were... I told her not to say anything, I wanted to /

B: You're a piece of shit.

Beat.

A: She made it to Miami. I don't know if you /

BEA shrugs.

B: Great.

Pause.

2.2.

A: How long have I got, more or less?

B: It's an estimate, so you have to take it with a pinch of...

109

She sighs. Reads.

Um. Schizophrenic symptoms should be kicking in now ish and then... You'll be lucky if you make it to fifty. And you'll have to hope your liver goes before Parkinson's sets in. Or that you're too deluded to care.

A: I'll nip it in the bud. When it gets too bad. When you get sick of me I'll disappear. You can send me to the knackers /

B: God don't say things like that! Fuck, Aaron! Fuck!

Pause.

Your mum didn't really get hit by a car did she?

A: Liver failure. She was an alcoholic.

B: And the money? The business didn't go bust.

A: It went on the /

B: Treatment. Care home.

AARON nods. BEA nods. Long pause.

A: I need to go see my /

B: You've let me feel smaller than you. Like I need to scrub up. Like your parents were these Gods on pillars, like I needed to check myself all the time in case you looked a bit closer and realised I wasn't good enough for you. I work so hard Aaron. And all this shit about not caring, 'Oh we're not ratists', that's all very well yeah, but you know mine's good! There were so many other men, so many other options, good, honest men with good blood. I had MyRate matches all the time, but I never followed them, obviously, because I chose you, some random man I met on a Wednesday afternoon. I thought it was romantic. Stupid! Fucking stupid!

Beat. She suddenly seems small.

I'm not ready for you to die.

A: I'm not dying.

B: But you will.

A: We're all dying. I'll probably just get on with it a bit faster than you.

B: And what about me? Am I supposed to watch you fade away, watch the last dregs of you disappear /

A: Schizophrenia doesn't work like that /

B: And then wait a couple of years for the rest of the shit to kick in so I can carry a shell of you to and from hospital until there's nothing left?

A: You'd do that for me wouldn't you?

B: Yes, of course I... I don't want to.

Pause.

You've murdered our child.

A: What?

B: I can't bring a sub into this world, it's not fair.

A: All the scans have been fine! We know it looks fine, we don't know, it might be /

B: I'm not creative like you. Can't draw for shit, make things, cook, whatever. But the idea I can make something good, something perfect, out of my body, our cells, I mean that's kind of incredible, I've never felt anything stronger, that feeling that we're building something perfect together. Not just the kid, but the next bit. It's a shitty world. It's so full of shit, you have to be...you have to be strong. And you have to plan. And you have to be right at the front from the start else it's really fucking tough. I've seen that. I've seen what it's like if you're not...perfect. I thought, I just thought...

She seems to be in physical pain. He goes to her. She flinches.

Go...do what ever you need to do.

A: Bea.

B: Get out. I need to... Just get out. GET OUT. GO AWAY. GET /

INTERLUDE 14

ON SCREEN: News footage. USA.

People queue. Others mill around, holding banners. Atmosphere of jubilation and almost religious fervour.

BRITISH BROADCASTER V.O.: ...outside Montgomery sterilisation clinic, where hundreds of sub-raters, encouraged by bystanders, are eagerly queuing, awaiting their turn.

A smiling women wears a t-shirt reading 'I am a vessel for the America of tomorrow' with an arrow to her womb.

Someone waves a banner reading 'Clean up our population. It's up to all of us'. Another: 'Contemplate the rate before you procreate'.

Cut to:

AMERICAN BYSTANDER: *(To camera.)* Yeah I'm just here to show my support. It's a very noble thing they're doing, and I hope every sub can be as selfless as these folk and do what's right to make our nation great again.

Back to crowd footage.

SCENE 14

Hospital corridor. Next day. Familiar soundscape. AARON sits holding a punnet of cherry tomatoes. He hasn't slept. BEA enters the hall. She sees him and freezes.

B: I'm working.

A: It's your lunch break.

Beat. He holds out the punnet.

I went to the shop across the /

B: Where did you stay?

A: Do you want to go and grab some food? We could go to the yellow...

BEA shakes her head. Beat. He approaches and touches her belly. She lets him for a moment, then removes his hand.

I'll come with you, if you want. To sort it out. If that's what you want to do. We can make another one, get high sperm obviously, but ours. Whatever you want. I'm sorry.

Pause. She stares at him. Mentally detaching herself.

B: I'll have my stuff out by the weekend.

A: No.

BEA turns to leave.

Hypocrisy's a fine thing.

B: Excuse me?

A: You /

B: *(Hissing)* Shut up you can't talk about that here.

A: Well then let's go /

B: No.

Pause.

Your rating will expire soon. Epigenetics. Lifestyle affects gene expression. I had to renew mine last month. Went down to 6.9, was shitting myself about telling you, isn't that hilarious? You'll lose your job. Your health insurance is gonna go through the roof.

A: I'll fake it again.

B: Even if you do, how long have you got left? Fifteen years? Twenty?

A: You said that's just an estimate.

B: It won't be long Aaron.

> *Beat.*

> When we got married I thought I knew what I was investing in.

A: What?

B: If you bet on something, put all your money on something, you'd want to know the odds, right? Or /

A: Bea /

B: Or, no, listen, or if you poured all your love, your life, into a, I dunno, a tree, a little pear tree, and you had to tend to it in the cold winter and dry summer, everyday, you'd wanna know if it was gonna wither away after a few years right? Or if it was gonna keep giving fruit?

A: Depends how sweet the fruit was.

B: I'm being serious.

A: So am I. I wouldn't want to know. I'd enjoy it while it lasted.

B: No, you would! And if it was diseased, you'd…

> *Beat.*

> I want to take it back.

A: What?

B: I don't want to invest any more love into it if it's gonna shrivel up, and I don't want to have to pay when it starts to /

A: Bea.

B: I don't want to. I can file for divorce on grounds of deception. I can find someone else, or I can just apply for sperm, maybe, or, I don't know /

A: We can do that, get in-vitro, obviously, but ours.

B: I don't want to! I don't want to suffer with you, watch you fade away, disappear, I've seen it before, it's not worth the...

A: Investment?

Beat.

B: Please just go.

Footsteps and muffled voices O.S. They look. DAVID enters. He stops.

D: Afternoon.

BEA nods.

A: Oh. Hi.

D: How's things?

A: Yeah, fine, yeah. Yourself?

D: Oh, same old. Same old. Can't complain. How's your father getting on?

A: Um. Yeah, OK, yeah.

D: Glad to hear it. Send him my regards.

BEA stares at DAVID. Silence. DAVID clocks the tomatoes.

Beautiful.

Beat.

Everything OK?

BEA stares at him. Beat. Nods.

Well, I'm on lunch. Do you two want anything from the...

Silence. BEA and AARON shake their heads.

Well, take care then.

He does his little bow. DAVID exits. Beat.

Dad used to be here in /

B: The psychiatric ward.

He nods.

Is he, um. OK?

A: Yeah. Stable. Thanks.

She nods. Beat.

'I hold it truth, whate'er befall; I feel it when I sorrow most; Tis better to have loved and lost, Than never to have loved at all'. Your favourite, right?

She looks at him calmly.

B: I've got savings. You can have the flat. The mortgage people will have a right shock. There's about sixty years left.

A: No. Please Bea, you can't. I'm sorry.

He tries to embrace her, to hold her belly.

B: Let me go.

A: Please.

B: Stop it.

A: I love you Bea, don't, please. I love you.

B: What does that mean? What's your love worth?

A: Bea.

B: 2.2. You are 2.2.

A: You love me.

B: Don't make this /

A: Please! Please!

B: I'm working.

A: Please!

B: Stop it.

She pushes him away, hard. The tomatoes roll in all directions.

INTERLUDE 15

AUDIO: Soundscape, A&E (sirens and chaos). Muffled voiceovers.

DR 1: ...just ran right out in front /

DR 2: ...a tram, right outside the /

DR 3: Intracranial hemorrhage /

DR 1: Unconscious, suspected bleeding to the /

DR 2: Well do we resus?

DR 3: What's the profile?

DR 1: Sub.

DR 2: If we're gonna /

DR 3: How low?

DR 1: 2.2

DR 2: We'd need to /

DR 3: No.

DR 2: Ok, move him on please!

Soundscape fades into:

SCENE 15

Hospital waiting room. A month later. A TV plays 'Wheel of Fortune'; the familiar V.O. plays into the empty room.

After a while, BEA enters slowly, carrying a newborn baby. DAVID enters after her.

D: He's beautiful.

Beat.

Why don't you sit down.

BEA nods, and sits down, holding the sleeping baby. DAVID exits.

I can give you a shout when they're ready to... It'll take a few minutes so you may as well relax eh. Well, you know the drill.

She watches the TV for a while, thinking. She brings the baby close to her. Her body is exhausted, but her brain is whirring.

BEA suddenly stands up, picks up her bag, carefully arranges the child, and makes for the other door.

DAVID enters.

D: They're ready for/

B: I. No, I don't want to know.

Beat.

D: You /

B: No...not yet. Thank you. I just want to look after him. For a bit.

BEA exits. DAVID watches her leave, then exits.

'Wheel of Fortune' continues to play into the empty waiting room.

CURTAIN.

WWW.OBERONBOOKS.COM